TARANTULA™ TRAIL

Weaving Excellence in a Connected World

SHANKAR NAGALINGAM
&
DR CHANTHIRAN VEERASAMY

INDIA • SINGAPORE • MALAYSIA

ISBN 979-8-89632-714-1

CONTENTS

AUTHOR BIO

Shankar Nagalingam, author of *Cheetah Chase: Sprinting Towards Success in the Global Business Jungle*, brings over 30 years of leadership expertise from Fortune 500 organizations. As a Vice President of Human Resources, a Prosci® certified change practitioner, Fellow Chartered Management Institute (CMI), United Kingdom and International Coaching Federation (ICF) Certified Coach. Shankar has established and led successful startup and shared services operations across Malaysia, fostering inclusive leadership throughout the APAC, US, and EMEA regions. His extensive experience in multicultural settings enriches his contributions to *The Tarantula Trail,* blending real-world insights with storytelling to make complex management ideas relatable.

Dr. Chanthiran Veerasamy, a seasoned Group CEO and Corporate HR Consultant, combines academic depth with practical experience. A Fellow Chartered Management Institute (CMI) United Kingdom, Certified as Senior Professional Human Resources (SPHR(i)). With certifications as a HRDF and CIPD Trainer, along with roles as Senior Lecturer and Adjunct Professor, Dr. Veerasamy has trained professionals across Fortune 500 companies, offering unique insights into strategic human resource management and organizational development.

His expertise adds a strong theoretical foundation to *The Tarantula Trail,* making the book an engaging guide for navigating today's professional landscape.

Together, Shankar and Dr. Veerasamy bring a shared vision of accessible learning through storytelling. *The Tarantula Trail* is designed to guide readers—from emerging professionals to experienced leaders—through the essential skills and adaptability required for success in an evolving business world.

AUTHORS NOTE

As authors of “The Tarantula Trail,” we are delighted to take you on a unique journey that weaves together professional insights with storytelling to illuminate the path toward future success. In an era where traditional career paths are rapidly evolving, we've chosen to break away from conventional management literature to offer something distinctively different – a blend of practical wisdom, future-focused skills, and engaging narrative that speaks to professionals at all stages of their careers and young adults stepping into the professional world.

Together, we bring complementary perspectives drawn from our diverse experiences in the corporate and academic worlds. One of us, Shankar Nagalingam, author of “Cheetah Chase: Sprinting Towards Success in the Global Business Jungle,” contributes over three decades of leadership experience in Fortune 500 multinational organizations, including expertise as a Vice President of Human Resources and Prosci® certified change practitioner. Through establishing and leading successful startup and shared services operations across Malaysia, this experience has fostered multicultural and inclusive leadership across APAC, US, and EMEA regions.

The other author, Dr. Chanthiran Veerasamy, brings both academic rigor and extensive corporate experience as a Group CEO and Corporate HR Consultant. With credentials as a Certified HRDF and CIPD Trainer, Senior Lecturer, and Adjunct Professor, this background adds a unique blend of theoretical foundation and practical application to our work. Years of training professionals across Fortune 500 companies have provided deep insights into the strategic aspects of human resource management and organizational development.

Our collaboration in "The Tarantula Trail" represents a shared vision of making complex management concepts accessible and engaging through storytelling. By interweaving fiction with practical insights, we aim to guide readers through the crucial skills and adaptabilities needed for future success. Whether you're a seasoned professional, a young adult starting your career journey, or someone seeking to understand the changing landscape of professional success, this book offers both wisdom and entertainment.

Through these pages, we invite you to follow an unconventional path – one that, like the tarantula's trail, may seem mysterious at first but leads to powerful discoveries about professional growth and personal development in our rapidly evolving world. We believe that the combination of our diverse experiences – spanning corporate leadership, academic research, and practical application – offers readers a unique perspective on navigating the challenges and opportunities that lie ahead.

We hope this journey inspires you as much as creating it has inspired us.

– Shankar Nagalingam & Dr Chanthiran Veerasamy

INTRODUCTION

Good day, everyone! This is your captain with a quick update. We're cruising at 35,000 feet, where it's a brisk -55°C outside—not exactly beach weather, right? Now, if you look out your window, you'll see our destination coming into view: ***Taranterra***. Yeah, that little dot surrounded by endless blue. Down there, it's a cozy 24°C—much better for a leisurely walk. We'll be touching down shortly at Whispering Winds Airport, where even the runway seems to hum with its own tune. So, tighten those seatbelts, folks! This isn't your average island. Taranterra plays by its own rules, and trust me, you'll want a front-row seat for this one.

In the middle of the Arachnid Ocean, where the waves move like they're whispering secrets to each other, sits Taranterra Island. It's not like any other place you've seen. The trees grow tall and twist in ways that make them look like they're reaching for the sky, and their leaves shimmer as if they're holding onto the last bit of morning dew.

This island is home to spiders that aren't just ordinary creatures. They spin webs that hold stories, secrets, and maybe even a bit of magic. These webs aren't just for catching bugs—they're threads that tie the whole island together, like a map of memories drawn in silk.

Taranterra is full of places that seem to have a life of their own. There's ***Mount Fanghorn***, where old spiders mumble to themselves like they're solving riddles. And then there are the ***Crystal Caves***, which glitter quietly, hiding more than they reveal.

The ***Whispering Woods*** is where stories hang on every branch. It's not just the wind that rustles through the leaves; it's the echoes of old tales, murmuring as though they've been caught in the trees themselves. This is where the young spiders come to learn their craft. They're taught to spin their first webs by the trees—yes, the trees—that seem to nod along, as if they know far more than they're letting on.

But Taranterra isn't all friendly whispers and gentle breezes. On the far side of the island lies the ***Quicksand Quagmire***. It's the kind of place that makes you stop in your tracks. The ground here moves like it's alive, swallowing everything in its path. They say the Sticky Sprites live there, tiny tricksters made of sap and shadow, always ready to lead the curious astray with a grin that says, "You should have known better."

And then, there's Spinneret Village, perched high in the branches of the Great Weeping Willow. It's not your usual village; these homes aren't built—they're woven, hanging lightly from the trees like they might float off if you weren't watching. Bridges made of silk stretch between them, swaying just enough to make you feel like you're dancing in the air. When night falls, the fireflies come out, turning the village into a little sky of its own, each light a tiny star caught in a web.

If you listen closely to the breeze in Taranterra, you might hear their names—eight ancient tarantulas, known as the Ancestors. Long ago, these ancient tarantulas shaped the land with their gifts, though their flaws left behind lessons just as important.

It's said that **Braxis** gave spiders their courage. His webs still hold the bridges of Spinneret Village, strong against any storm. But Braxis was reckless. He ventured too far into the Quicksand Quagmire, where the Sticky Sprites still whisper his name, daring others to follow in his steps.

Selendra understood the language of the trees. She taught the forest to remember stories, threading them into leaves that now rustle with forgotten tales. But Selendra trusted silence too much. She kept to herself, even when others needed her voice most.

Up in the peaks, **Fanghorn** watched over the land like a hawk. His sharp gaze let nothing slip by, and to this day, spiders say his spirit guards the mountains. But Fanghorn believed too much in strength, and his stubbornness left him lonely on the highest cliffs.

Mirren spun webs that told stories and dreams. Her threads were so perfect that some still drift through the air, catching fragments of forgotten hopes. Yet Mirren's love for perfection made her miss the beauty in things that weren't flawless.

The island's balance comes from **Ortho**, who knew that light and dark must always dance together. His wisdom lives in every decision the spiders make. But Ortho feared the future and spent too much time looking back, leaving others to move forward without him.

Zara kept the island connected, racing across the land faster than the wind. Her speed keeps the silk bridges strong, always carrying those brave enough to cross them. But Zara's impatience made her miss what truly mattered, leaving tangled threads behind her.

Nyro saw what others couldn't—glimpses of what might come. His visions still stir in the dreams of spiders, nudging them toward futures not yet written. But Nyro often doubted his own dreams, unsure if they were real or just fantasies spun from silk.

And then there was **Vexa**, who knew that darkness wasn't to be feared but embraced. She taught spiders that shadows bring rest and dreams. Yet Vexa kept too many secrets, and her silence made others misunderstand the importance of the night.

These eight ancestors—bold, silent, fierce, swift, wise, and flawed—wove the first threads of Taranterra. Their gifts shape the land, and their mistakes remind every spider that balance is the key to keeping the island alive. Their stories are everywhere: in the sway of Spinneret's bridges, the whispers in the woods, and the shadows that stretch across the land at dusk.

Even now, the spiders say the ancestors are never far away. Their spirits live in the wind, in the trees, and in every thread of silk spun on the island.

In this village, the spiders gather in the square, swapping stories and showing off the rare bugs they've caught from the furthest corners of the island. The young ones sit wide-eyed, drinking in every word. As the elders of Spinneret Village gathered in the glow of the fireflies, their voices rose in a soft, ancient song that drifted through the leaves:

"Spin the thread, weave the night,
Catch the dreams before they take flight."

They sang of webs that held more than silk, of stories that wrapped around the island like a silent promise. And for a moment, you could see it in the eyes of the young ones—that glint of curiosity that said they're already dreaming beyond the webs of their home.

At the center of the village square stood the Webclock. It wasn't just any old clock; this one had a way of catching the light like it was hiding a secret. They said its threads changed colors to match Taranterra's moods—sometimes glowing softly, other times pulsing like it had something important to say.

Just down the way was the Dewdrop Café, where the villagers went for a bite to eat. Nothing fancy, but you'd always find something tasty. There were honeydew shakes that made your legs tingle, muffins stuffed with juicy mosquitoes, and the famous Flutterby Flakes—crispy and sweet, just right to start the day.

Our story truly begins in a small cottage on the edge of this village. This is where Tara lived, a young spider whose presence was impossible to ignore. From the moment she hatched, everyone in the village knew she wasn't like the other spiderlings. Tara was a Goliath birdeater tarantula—the only one the island had seen in generations.She towered over the other spiders, her long, powerful legs covered in soft, reddish-brown hairs that glinted under the moonlight. Her body was larger, her frame broader, giving her an undeniable presence wherever she went. But it wasn't just her size that made her stand out—it was the way she moved. There was a restless energy in her every step, her legs twitching like they couldn't wait to take her somewhere new, as if adventure was calling her and she could never stay still for long.

Then there were her eyes—eight of them, each one bright and sharp, sparkling like tiny black jewels. Those eyes always seemed to notice things others missed. Whether it was the faintest shift in the breeze or a hidden path no one else had seen, Tara's gaze was always searching, always questioning, like she was looking for something just beyond reach.

In Spinneret Village, where most spiders were small and light, Tara's presence could feel overwhelming. Her size made it hard for her to weave between the branches as easily as the others, and she sometimes felt like she didn't quite belong. The other spiders were curious but kept their distance, unsure of what to make of her. Some whispered that she was a gift from the ancestors, others said she was a reminder of an older, wilder part of the island that had been forgotten.

Tara didn't mind standing out—not really. But there were moments when the weight of being different sat heavily on her. She often found herself gazing beyond the village, her legs twitching restlessly, feeling a pull toward the unknown. It was like the land itself was calling her, like the whispers in the woods and the hum of the crystal caves held answers she didn't yet understand.

And today, Tara was about to find out just how different she really was.

The morning sun slipped through her window, painting everything in a warm glow. Tara woke up feeling something was off—not wrong, exactly, but different. She couldn't shake the feeling that today was the beginning of something big. As she hurried downstairs, she found her adoptive parents, **Mr. and Mrs. Webber**, huddled close, talking in low voices over their cups of dewdrop tea.

"What's going on?" Tara asked, her eyes flicking from one to the other, trying to catch what they weren't saying.

Before Mrs. Webber could answer, a noise outside pulled her attention. The village was buzzing with whispers and excitement. Tara cautiously peeked out the window, curious to see what all the fuss was about. The noise had been growing louder, a mix of excited chatter and laughter. She brushed aside the curtain to get a better view, noticing a gathering of neighbors in the street, seemingly celebrating something that she had yet to understand.

In the center of the square, sitting proudly on a moth as large as a drifting cloud, was **Captain Arachnia Silkbeard**—the greatest explorer Taranterra had ever known. She wasn't just a tarantula; she was a legend, the kind whose name lived in hushed stories told under moonlight, passed from spider to spider like a precious secret.

Silkbeard belonged to the Silverfang Tarantulas, a species said to be born from the threads of fallen stars. The first of their kind were weavers who strung silk across endless skies, believing that to explore the unknown was to honor the stars from which they came. And Silkbeard carried that belief deep in her heart. Her beard—made of shining silver threads—wasn't just for show. Each strand, it was said, held a memory from an adventure, and her beard grew longer with every new place she conquered. Some even whispered that if you ran a leg through those threads, you could hear distant winds, the hum of waterfalls, or the creak of ancient trees she had discovered on her journeys.

But what made Silkbeard truly special wasn't just where she'd been—it was where she started.

Long ago, before she became a legend, she was just Arachnia, a little spider from the edge of the Quicksand Quagmire. Back then, she wasn't the fearless explorer everyone now knew. She was curious but small, and she often found herself tangled in her own webs—literally and figuratively. The other spiders laughed at her clumsy ways. They said she'd never weave anything but trouble.

Then, one stormy night, Arachnia wandered too close to the Quagmire, where the ground moved like a hungry beast waiting for its next meal. The storm's winds ripped her web to shreds, leaving her stranded on the slick, shifting sand. No one came to help. The villagers thought she was lost for good.

But Arachnia didn't sink. She spun.

Even with the storm howling and the sand pulling at her legs, she spun thread after thread, not to escape but to explore. She let the wind carry her silk across the Quagmire, catching onto branches she couldn't even see. And little by little, she made herself a bridge out of nothing but trust—trust in the wind, in her silk, and in herself. When the storm finally passed, Arachnia stood on the far side of the Quagmire, breathless and wild-eyed, staring at a land no spider had ever reached before.

That was the night she became Captain Silkbeard, the spider who learned that sometimes, the only way forward is to spin your web into the unknown. From then on, she vowed never to let fear stop her, no matter how tangled life got. Her silk became her compass, her beard a living map of all she'd discovered.

Now, whenever she returned to Spinneret Village, the spiders gathered like fireflies drawn to light, hoping to hear just a fragment of her latest tale. And today was no different.

"Gather 'round, everyone," she called, her voice steady but deliberate, each word landing with quiet force. "There's no time to waste."

The spiders shuffled closer, their eight eyes wide with unease. Silkbeard unrolled a large map, cracked at the edges and worn with years of travel. It was the kind of map that invited curiosity and dread in equal measure, full of places where secrets slept. She ran one leg over it, tapping different points with the precision of someone who had studied every path, every forest, every cave.

"Something is happening across Taranterra," she began, her tone measured but tense. "The Whispering Woods have fallen silent. Not a single story drifts through the leaves. The Crystal Caves, once alive with light, have dimmed. Even the waterfalls—the lifeblood of this island—are slowing to a trickle."

The crowd shifted uneasily, their voices rising in hushed whispers. Tara felt the hairs on her legs bristle. She didn't need the Captain to say more to feel the tension in the air. Something wasn't just wrong—it was spreading.

Silkbeard held up a leg to quiet the murmurs, her sharp eyes scanning the gathered spiders. "Listen closely," she said, lowering her voice until it was barely above a whisper. "This is no ordinary change. It's not just the forest or the caves fading away. There's a shadow moving across Taranterra, and it's not the kind that comes with night. It's older. Hungrier."

Tara's heart drummed faster, her legs twitching beneath her. She leaned in without meaning to, as if the weight of the Captain's words was pulling her closer.

“The shadow isn’t just taking things away,” Silkbeard continued, her voice tight with urgency. “It consumes—memories, stories, light. It leaves nothing behind, as if the land itself is being erased.”

The crowd went silent, the kind of silence that feels like holding your breath. Even the youngest spiders, who normally squirmed and fidgeted, stood frozen, their tiny legs still.

“There’s a pattern to it,” Silkbeard said, tapping the map with the tip of her leg. “The Whispering Woods... the Crystal Caves... the waterfalls. It’s not random. The shadow is moving with purpose, tightening its grip. It’s searching.”

A wave of uneasy murmurs spread through the crowd.

“Searching for what?” an older spider asked, his legs trembling slightly.

“For who?” came another voice from the back.

A mother spider pulled her young close, her voice rising with fear. “Is it after us? Should we flee before it reaches the village?”

“Where would we even go?” someone snapped. “The waterfalls are slowing, the caves are dimming—there’s nowhere safe left!”

“We need to warn the other villages!” another shouted, panic breaking in his voice. “The shadow will spread if they’re not prepared!”

"And what if it reaches the Spinneret first?" a black spider asked, her voice sharp. "They won't stand a chance without warning!"

"We should leave," a larger spider urged, already shifting toward the edges of the crowd. "We can go to the mountains—stay ahead of it before it finds us!"

"No!" hissed a grizzled elder. "You think the mountains are safer? Fanghorn's winds will throw you off the cliffs before the shadow even catches up!"

Another spider shouted, "We need to block the path to the Crystal Caves! If the shadow takes the crystals, there'll be no more light—nothing left for us to see or survive with!"

"What happens if the waterfalls stop entirely?" a young spider asked nervously. "Do we—do we dry out?"

The questions came faster, louder, each one feeding the growing fear. Legs twitched anxiously, and whispers rose like a buzzing storm. The spiders were panicking, trying to outthink a threat they couldn't see.

"Enough!" Silkbeard's voice snapped like a whip through the crowd, cutting off the rising chatter. The tension hung in the air, thick and oppressive, as every spider turned back to her.

"You can't outrun this," she said, her voice low and steady, carrying a weight that silenced even the boldest among them. "This shadow isn't a storm you can avoid or a predator you can fight. It doesn't just chase you—it feeds on your fear.

It twists what you leave behind—your regrets, your mistakes, your doubts—until there's nothing left of you."

A cold hush settled over the crowd, every spider still, as if even breathing too loudly might summon the darkness.

A gruff voice broke the silence. "So, what? We just wait to be consumed?"

A younger spider called out, frustration bubbling over. "How do we fight something we can't even see?"

"You fight it by holding on to what it cannot steal—what ties this island together," Silkbeard said, sweeping her gaze across the crowd. "It isn't the webs we spin or the places we hide—it's the stories, the memories, the light that lives inside us."

The spiders exchanged uneasy glances. Some shuffled their legs, unsure if they understood or if it was too late to try.

"But that won't be enough," a skeptical voice muttered from the crowd. "Memories and stories won't stop a shadow from swallowing us whole."

The murmurs grew louder, rising like a tide of panic.

"Why can't the Eight Ancestors help us?" a voice called from the crowd, sharp and desperate. "If they built this island, where are they now?"

"Yes!" another spider added. "They're the gods of Taranterra—why aren't they stopping this?"

The crowd buzzed with frustration and fear. Tara could feel the weight of their unease pressing in on her, like a heavy net she couldn't escape.

Captain Silkbeard's gaze hardened as she lifted a leg to silence them. "You think the Ancestors can save us?" she said quietly, her voice sharp and deliberate. "You think they haven't tried?"

The crowd fell into an uneasy hush.

"The Ancestors are not all-powerful," Silkbeard continued, her tone measured. "They wove the first threads of this island, yes. But they are bound by the balance they created—light and shadow, past and future, life and dreams. They don't rule over Taranterra. They exist within it, like currents in the ocean. And just as a wave cannot stop the tide, they cannot undo what is already in motion."

A tense silence followed as the spiders absorbed her words. Tara's heart drummed in her chest, and she leaned forward, sensing more to come.

Silkbeard's eyes flicked over the crowd. "The shadow that creeps across Taranterra isn't just darkness. It's old—older than the Ancestors themselves. It comes from a time before balance was found. A time when fear ruled and nothing was safe, not even dreams. The Eight Ancestors managed to hold it back once, but only just."

"But why didn't they destroy it?" a voice asked from the crowd.

Silkbeard shook her head. "Because this shadow isn't something that can be destroyed. It lives in the cracks of things—regret, fear, and forgotten stories. It thrives on what we leave undone. The Ancestors could only delay it, weaving the land with magic strong enough to hold it at bay for as long as possible."

Her gaze darkened as she scanned the map, tapping a spot where the Whispering Woods lay. "But now that magic is breaking. The balance they built is shifting. The shadow isn't just spreading—it's feeding on everything that was meant to hold it back."

Tara felt a chill crawl down her legs as Silkbeard's words settled over the crowd like mist. She knew, somehow, that the Captain was not just speaking of distant gods or ancient magic—this was about them, the creatures standing right here in Spinneret Village.

"And this is why the Ancestors cannot intervene," Silkbeard continued. "They created balance, but they cannot break it. That is not their role. They gave us the tools, the stories, and the light we carry inside—but the task of restoring that balance now falls to us. They cannot fight this shadow, because this is our battle."

A nervous spider in the front row shifted on his legs. "So... if the Ancestors can't stop it, what makes you think we can?"

Silkbeard's eyes landed on Tara, her expression calm but heavy with meaning. "Because the Ancestors left us something stronger than their magic. A piece of the island that even the shadow fears."

The Captain took a deep breath, as if the next words she spoke carried the weight of the world.

"A lost princess," she said, her voice dropping to a low, steady rhythm, as if the words themselves carried ancient power. "Hidden away when the shadow first stirred, protected from the darkness so she could return when the time was right. She carries the light we need—the light the Ancestors could not use."

The crowd exchanged hushed whispers, uncertainty flickering through their voices.

"She's the one the shadow fears," Silkbeard continued, "because she is the one who can do what even the Ancestors cannot. Not just fight the shadow—but restore what was lost. Reweave the threads of light and shadow into something new."

Tara stood frozen, her legs twitching beneath her. The words felt both foreign and familiar, as if they had been waiting for her all along.

"But where is this princess?" someone asked, confusion and hope mingling in their voice.

Just then, a strong gust of wind swept through the square, catching the Silkspinner's Clock off guard. Its threads began to glow brighter, twisting and turning until they formed the shape of a young spider—a spider that looked a lot like Tara.

Tara's eyes went wide, and for a second, it felt like the whole island was staring right at her.

All eyes were on Tara. She stood frozen, her legs trembling as Captain Silkbeard walked closer, her eyes steady and serious.

"Tara," the Captain said, her voice calm but firm, "it seems that your life is about to change in ways you never imagined."

Tara's hands shook as she reached out to take a small silk scroll from Mr. Webber. He placed it in her grasp with a look that wasn't just of worry—it was the kind of look a parent gives when they know something you don't, when they're holding onto a truth that will change everything. Tara's fingers fumbled as she unrolled the scroll, her eyes scanning the words that seemed to come alive on the silk:

"To our dearest daughter Tara,

There is so much you don't know about yourself, but the time has come for the truth. You are not just a spider of Spinneret Village; you are the lost princess of Taranterra. We hid you from the world to protect you from a darkness that once tried to consume our kingdom.

The same darkness is returning. It threatens to unravel everything we worked so hard to protect. We sent you to Spinneret Village so you could grow up far from danger, in the safety of kind hands and simple webs. But now, Taranterra needs you. We need you to become more than who you thought you were.

Go to the Whispering Willow in the heart of the Whispering Forest. It holds the first clue to your true purpose. You are meant to bring light back to this land, to stop the shadows before they destroy us all.

Be brave, be wise, and above all, trust in who you are meant to become.

With all our love,
Your true parents"

Tara's legs almost gave way beneath her. The words from the scroll wrapped around her like a net she couldn't escape. A princess? Her? She wasn't just Tara Spinner anymore; she was something much bigger, someone who mattered beyond her tiny corner of the village. She felt a mix of fear and a flicker of something else—something that felt like purpose.

She looked up at Mr. Webber, her voice shaking. "Why didn't you ever tell me?"

Mr. Webber's eyes were heavy with sadness. "We wanted to keep you safe, Tara. We promised your parents we'd look after you, that we'd let you be a child for as long as possible. They knew the world would be harsh when it found out who you really are."

Mrs. Webber stepped forward, her voice barely above a whisper. "Your real parents gave up everything to make sure you'd have a chance to grow up in peace. They believed that someday you'd find your way back when the time was right."

Tara's mind raced. She had always felt like she didn't quite fit in, like there was a bigger world she was supposed to be part of. And now that world was calling her, needing her to step into a role she never asked for. She wasn't ready, but the look in Captain Silkbeard's eyes told her that ready or not, her journey was already unfolding.

"You have a choice to make, Tara," Captain Silkbeard said. "Stay and live as you always have, or step into the unknown and fight for the kingdom you were born to save."

Tara's eight eyes looked out at the villagers who had gathered, all of them watching her with hope and worry. She realized that her journey wasn't just about finding herself—it was about protecting the place that had sheltered her, the people who had raised her as one of their own.

As the leaves of the Great Weeping Willow whispered in the wind, a song seemed to rise up from its branches, a song about courage, not of being fearless but of finding the strength to act even when you're scared. Tara knew then that her journey wasn't just a quest—it was a promise to the ones who believed in her, to the family that sacrificed everything to give her a fighting chance.

She stood taller, taking a deep breath. This wasn't just about being a princess. It was about saving the only home she'd ever known. And for the first time in her life, she felt a purpose that was bigger than her fears, bigger than her doubts.

And so, dear reader, the road ahead may be long and tangled, but every step Tara takes will be one filled with purpose. She's not just stepping into a story—she's stepping into her destiny.

CHAPTER 1

THE MIDNIGHT QUEST

Tara's head was still spinning from all that had happened. Captain Silkbeard's visit, the revelation that she was the lost princess of Taranterra—it was overwhelming. As she lay in her hammock, moonlight slipping through the silk-draped windows, her thoughts tangled like webs in the wind. The world she knew felt distant, and everything about her life had shifted in an instant.

Suddenly, a faint scratching at her window cut through the quiet. Then, a low, eerie voice followed.

"Tara… I'm coming for you..."

Her heart jumped to her throat. She shot up from the hammock, all eight legs braced to run. The voice deepened, dripping with over-the-top menace. "The shadows are here… and there's no escape!"

Tara grabbed the closest thing within reach—a rolled-up scroll—and held it like a weapon, her eyes wide as she stared at the window.

Just then, the "shadowy figure" outside let out a snorting giggle that shattered any sense of menace. The voice

THE MIDNIGHT QUEST

cracked mid-threat, and out popped Toby—grinning like a mischievous child caught in the act.

"Gotcha!" he cackled, clinging to the window ledge with an easy confidence. His whole body shook with laughter, and his dark-red knees glinted in the moonlight. "You should've seen your face, Tara! Priceless! Like, 'somebody call the ancestors because this girl's done!'"

"Toby!" Tara hissed, her relief turning to irritation. "You scared the silk out of me! What in the web are you doing creeping around like that?"

Toby wiped a tear from one of his eight bright eyes, struggling to catch his breath from laughing. His smile never faded, as if his entire existence was built on seeing how far he could push things. "How could I resist? You set yourself up, girl! I mean, that scream? Whew, I felt that!"

Tara crossed her legs in annoyance but couldn't keep a grin from tugging at the corner of her mouth.

"Come on now," Toby said, his grin widening. "Don't be mad. Life's too short for grudges. Besides, admit it—you like my dramatic entrance." He straightened up on the window ledge, putting on a mock-serious expression. "Was it creepy enough? Scale of one to 'I-need-new-bed-sheets,' what do you think?"

Tara rolled her eyes, but she couldn't help but laugh. "You're impossible."

"Impossibly charming, right?" Toby said, winking. "If I had a web for every time someone told me that, I'd have, well... a lot of webs." He placed a leg on his chest dramatically. "By the way, I didn't mean to catch you off guard like that. You know, Tara, if being a princess ever gets old, you could star in a horror play. I mean, your scream alone—legendary."

"You're ridiculous," Tara said, finally letting go of the scroll and setting it aside.

"And yet here you are, still talking to me." Toby grinned and gave her a playful wink. "Must mean I'm doing something right."

He leaned in a little closer, balancing effortlessly on the edge of the window. "So, you free tonight, or are you saving the world tomorrow? Because if you're not busy, I heard some buzzing over at Bugbite Café... Something about a secret meeting at Moonlit Hollow. Sounded like the kind of thing a princess and her charming sidekick should check out."

Tara raised an eyebrow. "Charming sidekick? Who says you get to be my sidekick?"

"Girl, I was born to be your sidekick," Toby shot back, flashing a toothy grin. "Fast, funny, great company—what more could you want?" He leaned in, his voice dropping to a mock-whisper. "Also, I look amazing in moonlight."

Tara laughed despite herself. "You're lucky I put up with you."

Toby shrugged, still grinning. "That's what makes us a great team. Now come on, Princess. Adventure waits for no spider! And let's be honest—you wouldn't survive five minutes out there without me."

Tara shook her head with a sigh, but her grin betrayed her amusement. "Fine. Let's go see what trouble you're dragging me into this time."

Toby gave an exaggerated bow, one leg sweeping dramatically. "As you wish, Your Royal Highness." Then he perked up, tapping the window ledge with a playful bounce. "But seriously, let's move before all the good drama's gone. Moonlit Hollow doesn't gossip about itself, you know!"

With a laugh, Tara climbed out of her hammock and followed Toby out the window, knowing full well that with him around, things were about to get much more complicated—and a lot more fun.

"Alright, let's go," Tara said. She wasn't sure she was ready, but she knew this was her first step toward understanding who she really was.

As they made their way through the silent village, every shadow seemed to stretch and sway, and Tara couldn't help but feel both fear and excitement. This was the kind of adventure she used to dream about, but now that it was real, it felt a lot more complicated.

They moved along the silken bridges, the gentle sway of the wind making the path feel more like a dance than a walk. Toby, as always, couldn't resist breaking the silence.

"So," Toby began, with that playful glint in his eyes, "how does it feel knowing you're a lost princess? On a scale of one to 'I-need-a-nap,' where are you at right now?"

Tara smiled despite herself. "Somewhere between 'I need a nap' and 'I want to hide under a rock forever.'"

Toby gave her an exaggerated look of sympathy. "Oof. Heavy stuff. But hey, at least you're not under some rock. You've got me. And I gotta say, you hit the jackpot—legendary sidekick and expert in making awkward situations less awkward."

Tara laughed softly but quickly grew quiet again, her eight legs moving slowly over the swaying bridge. "It's just... it's a lot, Toby. What if I mess this up? What if I can't be what they expect me to be?"

Toby glanced at her, the usual cheekiness in his expression softening. "You mean, what if you trip on your way to saving the world?" He nudged her with one leg, grinning. "We'll make sure it looks cool. But seriously, Tara, you've got this."

Tara let out a long breath. "I don't know, Toby. I mean, look at me. I'm this giant, awkward spider that barely fits into the village, and now I'm supposed to fit into some prophecy?" Her voice dropped, quieter now, as if the words were hard to say aloud. "What if... what if I'm too different? What if I don't belong anywhere?"

Toby stopped mid-step, turning to face her with a playful smirk. "Whoa, whoa, whoa—hold up. First of all, being different? That's, like, the coolest thing about you. You think being the same as everyone else makes a great princess? Nah. A princess has to be unforgettable." He leaned in with a mischievous glint. "And trust me, Tara, you are very unforgettable."

Tara gave him a side glance. "Is that your way of flirting or just cheering me up?"

Toby grinned, not missing a beat. "Why not both? Two for the price of one."

Tara rolled her eyes but couldn't hide the smile tugging at her mouth. "You're impossible."

"And yet," Toby said, dramatically placing a leg over his heart, "you still choose to hang out with me. Coincidence? I think not."

They walked in silence for a few more moments, the weight of Tara's thoughts still lingering. She glanced over at Toby. "What if I can't do this? What if I don't live up to the prophecy?"

Toby gave her a thoughtful look, dropping his usual grin for a rare moment of seriousness. "Listen, Tara. Prophecy or not, the only thing you have to live up to is being yourself. And you're already more than enough. Prophecies are just words—you make them real."

For a moment, Tara felt lighter. She had been carrying the weight of her doubts for so long, and here was Toby, somehow making them feel a little less heavy.

The two continued their way through the still night, the village now behind them. The soft hum of the Whispering Forest began to rise around them as they approached Moonlit Hollow, the edges of the trees glowing faintly from the light of strange mushrooms that circled the clearing.

"Almost there," Toby whispered. "And if anyone asks why we're late, let's just say we got tangled in adventure. Sounds cooler."

Tara smirked. "Toby, you'd get tangled in your own web if you weren't careful."

"True." He grinned. "But you'd still come untangle me, wouldn't you?"

Tara laughed. "Unfortunately for me, yes."

They reached the edge of the Moonlit Hollow, where the clearing opened into a perfect circle, glowing mushrooms casting a soft, otherworldly light that felt both calming and eerie.

Toby lowered his voice to a whisper. "You ready for this, Your Royal Highness?"

Tara took a deep breath, her legs steady now. "As ready as I'll ever be."

They crept closer, the low hum of voices drifting toward them like the first hint of a secret being revealed.

"Quick, hide!" Toby whispered urgently, yanking Tara behind a thick bush. His legs twitched nervously, but there was a glint in his eyes that suggested he was enjoying this a little too much.

Peering through the dense leaves, Tara squinted toward the clearing where a gathering of figures stood bathed in pale moonlight. There, at the center, was Madame Widow, the village's enigmatic fortune teller. The red and black patterns across her body gleamed under the night sky, giving her the appearance of something both beautiful and dangerous. Her legs moved slowly and deliberately, like a hunter weaving a web.

Beside her stood Old Thorax, the ancient insect whose droning stories were said to outlast lifetimes. His mandibles clicked quietly, and his wings drooped, as if the weight of time itself sat heavily on his back. Off to the side, almost invisible in the dim light, was Luna Glow, the quiet luna moth who rarely left her Misty Mountain home. Her wings shimmered faintly, like reflections of a forgotten dream, and even standing still, she looked as if she might vanish at any moment.

The night seemed heavier in the clearing, the air cold and unsettling, as if something unseen was pressing in from all sides.

"The signs are clear," Madame Widow said, her voice low and deliberate, the kind that seemed to wrap around your throat. Even the air seemed to chill with her words. "The Shadow Weavers are growing stronger every day. If the lost princess does not unlock the Twilight Codex soon... the island will be swallowed whole."

Tara's stomach knotted painfully. Twilight Codex? What was that? She'd never heard of such a thing before.

Old Thorax clicked his mandibles thoughtfully, his ancient voice crackling like brittle leaves. "The Codex has been lost for generations, buried in shadow and forgotten by time. How can we expect a young princess—barely aware of who she is—to succeed where so many have failed?"

Luna Glow shifted her wings, the faintest shimmer of light following her movement. Her voice, when it came, was as soft as a whisper riding on the breeze. "The prophecy is clear. The princess must face the three trials. Only by overcoming them will she be found worthy to wield the Codex's power."

Tara felt her mind spinning, her legs trembling beneath her. Trials? Prophecy? Her? The weight of it all was suffocating. She wasn't just someone out on an adventure anymore—she was Taranterra's last hope.

And then it happened. Toby shifted his weight, and the loud snap of a twig under his foot echoed through the clearing like a thunderclap.

The gathering froze. All eyes turned toward the bush where they hid. Madame Widow's gaze sharpened, narrowing like a predator catching the scent of prey.

"Who's there?" her voice sliced through the night, cold and demanding.

Tara's heart raced, pounding so loudly she thought the others might hear it. For a moment, panic clawed at her, begging her to run. But there was no running now. Not from this.

She took a breath—too sharp, too quick—then forced herself to step out of the bush, her legs shaky but steady enough. Toby shuffled behind her, whispering, "Well, this is awkward," as he tried to make himself as small as possible.

Tara stood tall, though her voice trembled slightly. "It's me," she said, her heart thudding in her chest. "Tara Spinner. Or... I guess, Princess Tara of Taranterra."

For a moment, the clearing was eerily silent. Then the three figures exchanged glances—an unspoken conversation passing between them—and, to Tara's utter disbelief, they bowed.

"Your Highness," Old Thorax said, the rasp in his voice softening with a respect Tara had never heard directed at her before. "We hoped you would find your way to us. There is much you need to learn, and little time to waste."

Tara stared at them, her breath catching in her throat. It felt like her whole life had been flipped inside out in a matter of hours. "Why didn't anyone tell me sooner?" she asked, her voice tight, cracking slightly. "How am I supposed to save an entire kingdom when... when I don't even know who I am?"

Madame Widow's many eyes softened as she stepped forward, her movements slow but deliberate, like every step carried the weight of centuries. One of her legs reached out and rested gently on Tara's shoulder. "Because, child," she said, her voice steady but kind, "you have always been more than what you believed yourself to be. Your parents knew it. They believed in you long before you knew how to believe in yourself."

Toby leaned in just enough to murmur, "I mean, no pressure or anything."

Tara shot him a side glance, trying to suppress a smirk, but the mention of her parents tightened her throat. She felt a knot twist inside her—her parents, a mystery she had never been allowed to solve. The mere thought of them made her feel small, like a spiderling who had wandered too far from the web. She swallowed hard, trying to push down the lump forming in her throat.

"But..." she whispered, the words fragile as silk, "what if I can't do this?" It wasn't just a question; it was a fear she had carried with her for longer than she wanted to admit.

Madame Widow tilted her head slightly, her gaze sharp and understanding, as though she could see through every doubt Tara carried. "You can," she whispered. "Because everything you need—every bit of magic, courage, and strength—already lives inside you. All you must do now is believe it, too."

Toby, standing just behind Tara, whispered under his breath, "Great, we're putting all our bets on self-belief now. That never goes wrong."

Tara threw him a look over her shoulder, half-exasperated, half-amused. "You're not helping, Toby."

"Helping is for amateurs," Toby whispered, grinning. "I'm here for emotional support and sarcasm. "

But beneath her irritation, Tara felt the slightest shift inside her—a flicker of something small but fierce. Determination. It was like finding a thread in a tangled web, a thread she wasn't ready to let go of.

Toby nudged her lightly. "Look, kid, if you can deal with me, you can handle anything. This whole 'save-the-kingdom' thing? Easy-peasy."

Tara huffed a quiet breath through her fangs, a small, sharp exhale that wasn't quite a laugh but close enough. "Do you ever take anything seriously?" she whispered, though the hint of fondness in her voice gave her away.

"Absolutely," Toby whispered back with mock sincerity. "Just not before midnight."

Tara clicked two legs together, a habit she'd developed when she was trying not to smile. Toby caught the movement and grinned triumphantly. "See? You're already feeling better. This is why they keep me around."

Tara gave him a quick glance, this time full of meaning. "I keep you around to stop you from getting yourself squashed."

"Details," Toby replied, shrugging one of his knees dramatically. "I like to think of it as character-building."

Old Thorax clicked his mandibles, drawing their attention back to the gathering. "The shadow grows closer with every moment we stand here. This reunion is charming, but the time for jokes is over." His voice buzzed with the weight of centuries, as though the entire forest was holding its breath along with him.

Tara looked at Madame Widow, Old Thorax, and Luna Glow—their faces lined with years of knowledge, hope, and fear. They weren't just waiting for her to succeed—they were depending on her. The fate of Taranterra rested in her legs.

She wasn't ready. Not yet. But that didn't seem to matter anymore.

Tara nodded, her jaw tight but steady. "I'll try," she said quietly, her voice filled with a fragile but growing strength. "Not just for me. For the village... for the island."

A hint of approval flickered in Madame Widow's many eyes. "Good," she said. "Because, young princess, the trials are only the beginning. The shadow waits. And now, so do we."

For the next hour, Tara sat in stunned silence, her legs drawn close beneath her as the elders' voices filled the clearing like threads of an ancient web being rewoven. The moonlight glimmered off Madame Widow's glossy markings, making her presence feel larger than life, as if the night itself leaned in to listen.

"The prophecy is older than any of us," Madame Widow began, her voice as smooth and cold as silk sliding across stone. "It tells of a time when Taranterra's balance will be shattered, and only the lost princess—hidden from the shadow's grip—can restore what has been broken."

Tara's heart drummed against her ribs, each beat heavier than the last. It was one thing to hear whispers of a prophecy, but it was another to hear it laid bare before her, every word wrapping around her like a shroud.

Old Thorax let out a slow, deliberate buzz, his mandibles clicking with ancient weariness. "The princess must face three trials," he rasped. "Each trial tests a part of her soul—a part the shadow will exploit if she fails."

Tara shifted uncomfortably, her legs twitching against the ground. She wanted to ask questions, to slow the rush of overwhelming information crashing over her, but the elders pressed on.

"The first is the The Trial of the Eldritch Flame," Madame Widow continued, her many eyes gleaming as if they saw far beyond the present. "Deep within the Echoing Caves, you will face your fears. The caves show you what you dread most—whether it's real or not, you won't know until it's too late."

Tara felt a chill run down her spine, the weight of her insecurities pressing down like a storm cloud. What would the caves show her?

"And the second?" Tara asked, her voice quieter than she intended.

Old Thorax gave a slow nod. "The Oracle's Enigma," he buzzed. "At the peak of Mount Fanghorn, where the winds scream through the cliffs, you will have to make choices. Some will seem right but lead you astray. Others will appear impossible, yet they will be the only way forward."

Tara's legs stilled, the gravity of it all sinking deeper into her bones. It wasn't just physical strength they wanted from her—it was her mind, her judgment, her ability to see beyond the obvious. And what if she got it wrong? What if she chose wrong and there was no second chance?

"And the last trial?" she whispered, almost afraid to hear the answer.

Luna Glow, who had been quiet until now, fluttered her wings softly, her glowing presence eerie but calm. "The final trial," she said, her voice so soft it was barely more than a sigh, "is The Quest of Open Hands," in the heart of the Quicksand Quagmire. There, you will be tested not by what you do for yourself, but what you are willing to sacrifice for others."

Tara's throat tightened, and a knot formed in her stomach. The thought of those treacherous sands—always shifting, always pulling everything down into the dark—made her legs ache just thinking about it. What would she have to give up? How far would she have to go for others?

Madame Widow's gaze darkened, her voice carrying a solemn warning. "Each trial will push you to your limit.

They are not designed to test your strength alone, but your heart, your choices, and your resolve. If you fail…" She paused, letting the words hang in the cold night air. "The shadow will grow stronger, and you will be lost within it."

Tara swallowed hard, her breath shaky. The enormity of it all pressed in on her, the weight of the prophecy settling on her shoulders. It was no longer just about discovering who she was—it was about becoming someone who could carry the fate of an entire kingdom.

For a moment, the fear surged, threatening to pull her under. "What if I can't do it?" she asked quietly, her voice wavering. "What if I fail?"

Old Thorax gave a slow, thoughtful click, his gaze heavy with age and understanding. "Every creature faces failure at some point, child," he said, his voice a low drone. "But the real test lies in what you do after. Courage isn't about never being afraid—it's about moving forward even when fear has taken hold of you."

Luna Glow fluttered her wings again, her soft glow illuminating Tara's uncertain expression. "The trials will reveal who you truly are," she whispered gently. "Not the princess the prophecy speaks of, but the Tara beneath the crown."

Madame Widow leaned closer, her many eyes sparkling with a calm curiosity. "You have always been more than what you believed yourself to be. The question is not whether you are ready, but whether you will choose to rise."

Tara looked from one elder to the next, her heart pounding, her mind racing. Every doubt she had ever carried—every fear, every insecurity—was screaming at her to run, to hide, to pretend none of this was happening. But beneath all that noise, something quiet but steady began to stir—a flicker of determination, small but growing.

She could feel it now. This wasn't just a test for her. It was for everyone—the village, the forest, the caves, and everything she held dear. There was no one else who could take her place. This was her path, whether she felt ready or not.

"Okay," she whispered, more to herself than anyone else. "I'll try."

Old Thorax inclined his head, his mandibles clicking with approval. "Good," he said. "Because once the trials begin, there is no turning back."

Madame Widow's voice lowered, soft but firm, like the final knot in a web. "The shadow is already stirring, child. Time is not on your side."

Tara's breath hitched, and the night seemed to press in closer, heavier. But beside her, she felt a spark of something strange—something almost like hope.

"And remember this, young princess," Luna Glow added, her voice drifting like the last breeze of summer. "The trials do not test your perfection. They test your heart."

Tara stood slowly, her legs steady beneath her. For the first time since stepping into the clearing, she felt not just the weight of fear—but the pull of purpose.

"Then I guess I don't have a choice," she whispered, her voice barely audible.

Madame Widow gave a slow, deliberate nod. "You never did."

Toby, who had been unusually quiet through the entire exchange, shifted beside Tara, his bright eyes wide with disbelief. He opened his mouth, closed it, then finally leaned closer, whispering just loud enough for her to hear.

"Okay, so... no pressure or anything, right? Just save the whole island and face certain doom. Piece of cake." He paused dramatically, one leg tapping the ground. "I mean, why didn't they throw in, I don't know, taming a dragon while they were at it? Or maybe a dance-off with the shadow for good measure."

Tara tried to suppress a laugh, but it escaped, a small puff of breath in the tense night air. She needed that, and Toby knew it.

"By the way, have you noticed these folks talk like they're narrating the end of the world? Like, could we maybe tone down the doom and gloom just a little?"

Luna Glow's soft wings fluttered, and Toby shot her an awkward smile. "No offense, Luna. Your vibe is... peaceful and mysterious, I get that. But these trials sound like they were cooked up by someone who really hates spiders."

Tara rolled her eyes, though there was warmth behind it. "I think we've got bigger things to worry about, Toby."

He straightened, legs shifting into a mock-heroic stance. "Bigger than me being the comedic backbone of this operation? Unlikely." Then, with a small smirk, he leaned in closer, dropping his voice to an almost conspiratorial whisper. "But seriously, Tara... you've got this. I mean, look at you—you've been carrying the weight of being different your whole life. What's a little prophecy compared to that?"

Tara's eyes softened. Toby had this way of taking something overwhelming and shrinking it down until it felt manageable—like the shadow wasn't quite so big, the trials not quite so impossible.

"Thanks, Toby," she said, and for the first time that night, her voice didn't waver. "But if I'm doing this, you're coming with me."

Toby grinned wide. "Well, obviously. I didn't sneak out of my hammock to let you hog all the adventure. Someone's gotta make sure you don't accidentally hero yourself into a mess you can't climb out of."

Madame Widow cleared her throat, giving Toby a look sharp enough to cut silk. "The trials are no joke, young one. This is not a game."

Toby held up his legs in mock surrender, still grinning. "Oh, no disrespect, Madame. I'm just saying—if Taranterra's gonna be saved, it'll take more than just doom-filled prophecies. It's gonna need some charm, too. And luckily for her"—he gave Tara a playful nudge—"I've got plenty to spare."

Tara shook her head with a sigh but couldn't help the smile spreading across her face. With Toby at her side, the trials ahead still felt daunting—but just a little less terrifying.

As the meeting ended, the elders drifted into the shadows, their forms dissolving like mist caught in moonlight. Madame Widow's many eyes blinked one last time, and with a faint hum, she seemed to fold into the night itself, leaving only a cold breeze in her place. Old Thorax gave a final, low click of his mandibles, his wings buzzing softly as if carrying secrets on the wind, and then vanished without a sound. Luna Glow's wings shimmered, flickering like a dying star, before she too melted into the shadows, as if she had never been there at all. The clearing was empty in seconds, leaving only the soft rustling of leaves—and the weight of everything they had said—hanging in the air.

Tara shivered slightly, the quiet pressing in around her. "They sure know how to make an exit," she muttered, trying to shake off the lingering sense of unease.

"Yeah, 10 out of 10 on the spook factor," Toby whispered, his eyes darting around, half-expecting the elders to reappear out of nowhere. "I'm just saying—no way I'm ever playing hide-and-seek with those folks."

They began making their way back toward Spinneret Village, the night starting to give way to the first light of dawn. A pale glow spread across the horizon, making the silken paths shimmer underfoot. Tara's mind churned with everything she had heard—prophecies, trials, shadows creeping closer. The weight of it felt heavy on her chest, like she was walking with an invisible burden she couldn't shake.

Toby glanced at her from the corner of his eye. "You've got that look again," he said, his voice softer this time. "The one where your brain is spinning webs faster than you can untangle them."

Tara exhaled, her legs moving slowly along the path. "It's just... a lot, you know?"

Toby stepped a little closer, his usual grin softening into something gentler. "Hey, you don't have to carry all of it alone, you know. That's kind of why you've got me. The charmingly annoying best friend with impeccable timing."

Tara gave him a sideways glance, a small smile tugging at her mouth. "Is that your way of saying you're useful?"

Toby puffed out his chest, the red markings on his knees catching the faint light. "Not just useful—irreplaceable. And handsome too. If I weren't such a gentleman, I'd say the prophecy should've been about me."

Tara let out a breathy laugh, her first real laugh in what felt like hours. "Oh, please. You'd trip over your own legs five minutes into the first trial."

Toby grinned, leaning just a little closer. "Ah, but wouldn't it be worth it if it made you laugh?"

The way he said it, light and playful but with a hint of sincerity, made Tara's heart stutter for half a beat. She bumped him lightly with her leg, but the warmth in her chest lingered.

They walked in silence for a little while, the village now coming into view, the branches of the Great Weeping Willow swaying gently in the morning breeze. As they neared Tara's house, the sky glowed a soft pink, the first signs of day breaking over the horizon.

Just as Tara was about to climb back into her window, she froze. Something wasn't right. A soft, golden glow caught her eye from inside the room.

Toby noticed it too. "Whoa... Did you leave a nightlight on, or are we about to be visited by more creepy fortune-telling ghosts?"

Tara raised a brow at him but leaned through the window cautiously. There, on her pillow, lay a small, finely woven silk pouch. The threads shimmered faintly in the soft light. Slowly, she opened it, and inside was a single, glowing feather, so delicate it looked like it might dissolve into the air. It pulsed with a soft, warm light that made her chest feel lighter, like it was chasing away the heaviness that had followed her since the meeting.

Nestled beneath the feather was a small note, written in thin, looping script:

"For when the darkness feels too heavy. Use it wisely."

Toby peered over her shoulder, his face close to hers. "That... is the fanciest feather I've ever seen. And I've seen a lot of feathers. Think it does magic stuff? Or just makes pillows extra comfy?"

Tara traced a leg lightly over the glowing feather, her heart warming despite everything weighing on her. "I think it's more than just decoration," she murmured.

Toby leaned closer, his voice low and teasing. "You know, Tara, if you get all serious on me now, I might have to steal that feather and use it to tickle you back to normal."

Tara laughed, a real, unguarded laugh that felt better than she expected. "You'd better not."

"Try and stop me," Toby whispered playfully, his grin wide. "I'm faster than I look."

She gave him a playful swat with one leg, and he pretended to stumble backward dramatically, clutching his chest. "Wounded! By a princess no less! And here I thought we were building a moment."

Toby had a way of turning even the heaviest moments into something lighter, something bearable.

She tucked the feather into her pack and rested her head against the edge of the hammock, her gaze lingering on Toby for a moment longer than usual. "Thanks," she said softly.

Toby grinned, his bright eyes glinting in the early morning light. "Anytime, Princess. Now try not to get all emotional on me. Can't have you falling for me before the first trial starts—people will talk."

Tara let out a huff, but she couldn't help the small smile that stayed on her face as she lay back in her hammock. The feather glowed faintly in her pack, its light a quiet reminder that even in the darkest moments, there was always something waiting to lift her up. And Toby, with all his jokes and charm, was already proving to be one of those things.

Outside the window, Toby gave a playful wave with one of his front legs, the same mischievous grin plastered across his face. "First light, Princess. I'll be here. Don't keep destiny waiting, alright?"

Tara chuckled softly, leaning back into her hammock as the glow of the feather pulsed gently from her pack. For the first time that night, the future didn't feel quite so overwhelming. With Toby's unwavering presence—and that ridiculous charm—beside her, she felt ready to face whatever the dawn would bring.

But deep within the twisted tunnels of the Crystal Caves, where light dared not venture, a different kind of darkness stirred. The air was thick and cold, clinging to the stone walls like a breath that refused to leave. Shadows didn't just sit there—they moved, twisting and writhing as if they had minds of their own. And at the center of it all stood Lord Nightweaver.

He was more than just a shadow himself; he was the darkness given form, his eyes burning like two sickly yellow embers in the pitch-black. His silk wasn't like the others'—it glistened with an oily sheen, threads that seemed to drink in the light and spit out darkness. He stood motionless, yet everything around him felt like it was alive and seething, like the cave itself was holding its breath.

"The lost princess has returned," Nightweaver hissed, his voice like a hundred whispers layered on top of each other, echoing off the cavern walls. "She thinks she's ready to face us." He let out a slow, joyless chuckle, the sound bouncing off the cold stones, making even the bravest of his followers shudder.

"She has no idea," he continued, his eyes narrowing into slits, "that this island belongs to the shadows now. She won't reach the Twilight Codex. We'll bury her dreams and that foolish prophecy in darkness so deep, not even her light can find it."

The Shadow Weavers, his loyal followers, huddled close, their forms flickering like smoke caught in the wind. They nodded and murmured in agreement, their eyes reflecting a twisted devotion. Nightweaver's gaze swept over them, and with a flick of his many legs, he summoned a thick, swirling mist—a black fog that seemed to pulse with a life of its own.

"Prepare the Shadowmist," he commanded, his voice sharp and cold. "Let it spread across Taranterra. Let it seep into every web and every hollow. Let the island choke on its own fear."

As the mist began to curl and twist through the tunnels, creeping into every crack like a living thing, Lord Nightweaver's smile grew. It wasn't a smile of joy or even victory—it was the smile of someone who enjoys tearing hope apart, thread by thread.

"Taranterra thinks a princess can save them?" he whispered, his voice barely more than a breath, but powerful enough to freeze the very air around him. "We'll show them what it means to fear the dark."

Just as the Shadowmist began its slow crawl across the land, painting the island in shades of dread, the first rays of dawn touched Spinneret Village. Tara woke with the weight of the night still pressing on her, but there was something stronger inside her now—something that burned brighter than her fear.

She stood tall, gripping her magical items, her eyes fixed on the horizon where the Whispering Willow awaited. The doubts, the worries, the fear—they were still there, but they were smaller now, quieter. She looked to Toby, who watched her with wide, hopeful eyes, and then she turned her gaze to the woods ahead, knowing that whatever came next, she wouldn't face it alone.

"The darkness may be strong," Tara said, her voice steady and clear, "but it's not stronger than the light we carry inside us. Taranterra needs me, and I won't back down. And with that, Tara took her first step into the unknown, not just as a spider or a princess, but as the light that Taranterra needed to face its darkest hour.

CHAPTER 2

FRIENDS IN UNLIKELY PLACES

As the first light of dawn spread across Spinneret Village, turning everything soft shades of pink and gold, Tara set out on her journey. She tried to ignore the knot of nerves twisting in her stomach. Today was the day. She wasn't just Tara Spinnerling anymore; she was the lost princess of Taranterra, and she had a kingdom to save. With the mysterious feather from last night tucked safely in her pack, she took a deep breath and glanced at Toby, who was already bouncing on his many legs.

"Alright, Toby, here we go," she said, her voice both determined and shaky.

"That's the spirit!" Toby replied, giving her a playful salute. "Adventure calls, and we must answer!"

They left the safety of the village and made their way toward the Whispering Woods, which marked the border between what was familiar and the unknown. The trees of the forest stood tall and twisted, their branches like long fingers reaching out to touch the sky. The air felt different here,

THE TARANTULA TRAIL

thicker, as if the forest itself was watching them, holding its breath.

"Kind of feels like we're stepping into someone's secret," Toby said, glancing around with wide eyes. "I mean, if these trees start whispering, I'm out of here."

"It's called the Whispering Woods for a reason, Toby," she said, trying to sound braver than she felt. "Let's hope they're friendly whispers."

As they ventured deeper into the woods, the sights and sounds of the village faded away, replaced by things both strange and wonderful. Butterflies with wings that tinkled like tiny bells fluttered past, and flowers that seemed to change colors with every breeze nodded to them as if in greeting. For a moment, Tara felt like they had stepped into a world that was alive in ways she had never known.

Toby nudged her with a grin. "See, this isn't so bad! Magical flowers, chiming butterflies—this is practically a vacation! All we need now is a hammock and some snacks."

Just as Tara and Toby were making their way through the forest path, a sudden puff of purple smoke exploded in front of them.

"Whoa!" Toby yelped, hopping back as something tumbled out of a lopsided treehouse perched precariously above them.

A large, friendly-looking tarantula rolled to a stop at their feet, coughing dramatically and batting out a small flame still smoldering on one of his legs. His bristly, chocolate-brown legs contrasted with bright yellow patches around his joints, giving him a bold, striped appearance.

"Oh, beetle legs and cricket guts!" he groaned, adjusting his oversized goggles. "Third explosion today! I'm either getting better at this or much worse."

Tara stifled a laugh, raising one eyebrow. "Who are you?"

The tarantula straightened up, gave them an exaggerated, elegant bow, and puffed out his chest. "I am Andy—scientist, genius, occasional fire hazard, and inventor extraordinaire! At your service." He grinned, flashing fangs that somehow managed to look friendly. "And who might you be, oh curious wanderers?"

Before Tara could speak, Toby stepped forward with a smug grin. "Hold on, hold on. We've got a princess in the house, Andy! Try not to trip over your stripes in excitement."

Andy leaned in with a playful smirk. "A princess, huh? Must be your lucky day, Toby. Usually, it's you who scares everyone away."

Toby snorted. "Me? Scare them away? Please, they run because they can't handle this much charm."

Andy chuckled, adjusting his goggles. "That's one way to put it. Though, let's be real—you're more of a warning sign than a welcome mat."

Toby gave him a mock bow. "I see you're quick with the insults. I respect that."

Andy winked. "Years of practice."

Tara shook her head, amused by their playful banter. "Is this how it's going to be the entire time?"

"Absolutely," Andy said with a grin. "But hey, you need the comic relief. If you didn't, Toby would have been replaced by now."

Toby raised a leg dramatically. "You know what? I'll allow it—only because you're the one who's going to explode something, not me."

"Correction," Andy said, brushing soot off his front legs. "That was a minor miscalculation. This time, my newest creation is totally foolproof."

Toby crossed his legs skeptically. "The same foolproof that just blew up your treehouse?"

Andy grinned. "Science is all about experimentation. And explosions. Mostly explosions."

Tara laughed, the weight of the day lifting just a little. "Do you always manage to blow something up before introductions?"

"Only when I want to make an impression," Andy replied. "Now, let's focus. If you two are on a quest, you'll need all the help you can get—and lucky for you, I've just finished fine-tuning my greatest invention!"

With a dramatic flourish, Andy pulled out a glowing metal device from his satchel. "Behold! The Lumin-Essence

Detector. It picks up traces of magical energy—like a compass, but with sparkles."

Toby arched an eyebrow. "And it won't, you know, explode or summon angry moths?"

"That was one time!" Andy said, feigning offense. "And for the record, it wasn't my fault the moths had unresolved anger issues."

Toby snickered. "Sounds like something I'd hear from someone who just barely made it out alive."

Andy wagged a leg at him, grinning. "Surviving is the mark of genius."

Just as the purple smoke cleared and Andy dusted himself off, Tara gave him a curious look. "Wait, how did you know we're on a quest?"

Andy grinned, adjusting his soot-covered goggles with flair. "It wasn't hard to guess. A princess sneaking around in the dead of night with a sidekick? Definitely quest vibes."

Anyway, the real question is—what's the quest? Spill it. I'm all ears... and legs."

Tara hesitated for a moment. She wasn't sure if they could trust Andy yet, but he seemed more enthusiastic than anyone she'd met so far. She glanced at Toby, who gave her a small shrug, as if to say, Might as well.

"Fine," she said, taking a deep breath. "There's an old prophecy... one that says I'm a lost princess—Taranterra's only hope. But to save the island, I have to pass three trials. The first one is at the Echoing Caverns."

Andy's eyes widened, and for a moment, he was speechless. "Wait—you're the lost princess? No way. That is... amazing!" He bounced slightly, excitement bubbling over. "Do you have, like, a crown somewhere, or is that still pending?"

"No crown," Tara muttered. "Just a lot of responsibility."

"Responsibility's overrated," Andy replied with a wave of his leg. "But a prophecy? That's the good stuff." He leaned in closer, his grin widening. "You know, I'm an expert in quests. Pretty sure the first rule is you're not allowed to go on one without me."

Toby gave him a skeptical look. "Oh yeah? And what makes you quest-worthy?"

Andy smirked, brushing off more soot from his leg. "For starters, I have a device that can detect dark magic—something tells me that's gonna come in handy."

Toby narrowed his eyes. "Unless it explodes."

Andy gave a mock gasp, clutching his chest dramatically. "You wound me, Toby. One small mishap, and suddenly I'm unreliable?"

Tara shook her head, biting back laughter. "Well, at least you'll keep things interesting."

Andy winked. "Exactly. And who knows, Princess? Maybe I'll save the day, and you'll end up writing songs about me."

Toby gave a playful shove with his leg. "Yeah, she'll write songs about your spectacular failures."

"Failures are just success in disguise," Andy quipped, not missing a beat.

"Wow," Toby muttered, impressed. "You're good."

In the short time they'd known Andy, he had already managed to lift some of the weight off her shoulders. Maybe this ridiculous, brilliant tarantula would be exactly what they needed to survive the trials.

They continued deeper into the forest, the trees thickening and shadows stretching across the path. Andy chattered away about his inventions, each story more ridiculous than the last.

"There was that time I invented an umbrella that doubles as a parachute," Andy said proudly. "Worked perfectly—until the wind caught it and sent me headfirst into a river."

Toby snorted with laughter. "Please tell me there's a fish story involved in this."

"Three fish, actually," Andy said with a grin. "Two swam away in shock, but the third tried to eat my goggles."

Toby shook his head, still laughing. "You're a walking disaster. I like you."

"Thanks. You're not so bad yourself, Mr. Charm Factory," Andy quipped, giving Toby a playful nudge.

The light-hearted banter was cut short when the forest suddenly grew eerily quiet. The colorful flowers along the path drooped, their vibrant petals fading to dull grays. Even the sun seemed to struggle to pierce the canopy, casting only dim, weak beams onto the forest floor.

Toby froze, his cheerful demeanor evaporating. "Okay, I'm officially not loving this vibe anymore."

Tara's senses sharpened as her legs tensed beneath her. "Something feels... wrong."

Andy pulled out his Lumin-Essence Detector, the glow from the device flickering like a dying ember. "There's a surge of dark energy nearby," he whispered. "Stay sharp. This isn't the friendly kind of magic."

Just then, a low, bone-chilling laugh echoed through the trees, making the air feel colder. From the shadows of a twisted, ancient tree, a figure stepped forward, its body a swirling mass of smoke and darkness. Its eyes glowed an unnatural green, and its legs slithered forward like coils of shadow, as if it wasn't fully solid.

Toby let out a nervous squeak. "Uh, please tell me this is one of your inventions, Andy."

Andy's eyes widened behind his goggles, but his voice stayed calm. "Nope. That's not mine. That's pure, unfiltered evil."

Toby gave a nervous chuckle, though it didn't hide the fear in his voice. "Fantastic. Just what I wanted—an adventure with optional nightmares."

Andy flicked the switch on his detector, which glowed brighter but gave off an alarming hum. "Well, lucky for us, I've got some tricks. But, uh... you two might want to start running—now."

Tara didn't need telling twice. "Go!" she whispered urgently, as the shadowy figure hissed and began to glide closer.

Toby shot Andy a panicked look. "If we die, I'm haunting you."

"Deal," Andy quipped, grinning despite the danger. "But you better keep up, or you'll miss all the fun."

And with that, the three of them sprinted down the darkened path, with the sound of twisted laughter chasing close behind.

The figure that stepped out of the darkness was a spider, but not like any Tara had ever seen before. Its body seemed to be woven from shadows, constantly shifting and twisting like smoke that couldn't decide which way to go. Its eyes glowed with an eerie purple light, almost as if they were looking straight into her soul.

"Well, well, well," the shadowy spider said, its voice smooth and cold, like ice sliding down a wall. "What do we have here? A lost little princess and her two clueless friends stumbling through my forest?"

Tara's heart thumped loudly in her chest, but she forced herself to stand tall, even though her legs felt like they might give way. "We're not afraid of you!" she said, her voice shaking just a little.

The spider's smile stretched wider, its teeth sharp and glistening. "Oh, but you should be," it hissed. "I am Shade, the right hand of Lord Nightweaver. And I'm afraid your little quest ends right here."

Shade's smile twisted into something even more menacing as its shadowy tendrils slithered forward, wrapping around Tara, Toby, and Andy. The air seemed to grow colder, each breath feeling like ice settling into their lungs. The darkness didn't just surround them—it pressed in, squeezing tight, draining the light from their very souls.

"Tara!" Toby yelled, his voice trembling as he swatted helplessly at the tendrils. "I've had enough of this creepy stuff! Any bright ideas—literally?!"

Andy, usually so full of quirky confidence, was now shaking like a leaf, his legs trembling uncontrollably. "I-I'm an inventor, not a warrior!" he stammered, his goggles fogging up with panic. "This isn't in my job description!"

The shadows crawled up her legs, cold and suffocating, like they were feeding off her fear. Her legs felt like they were frozen in place.

Shade's laughter echoed through the clearing, low and cold. "What's wrong, little princess?" it taunted, leaning closer, its eyes burning with a sinister purple light. "Lost your courage? This is how it ends—caught in the dark, where you belong."

Tara felt her hope slipping away, the light in her heart flickering like a dying candle. She thought of everything—the prophecy, her parents, the kingdom depending on her—and the weight of it all seemed too heavy to bear. Her hands moved instinctively to her pack, desperate for something, anything, that could help.

And then it happened.

A warm glow pulsed from inside the pack. The mysterious feather burst into light, brighter than anything they had ever seen. It wasn't just a glow—it was a fierce, blazing light that seemed to come from deep within, like the sun itself had been reborn in that tiny feather. The darkness recoiled, the tendrils shrinking back as if burned by the sheer force of the light.

Toby's eyes went wide, his mouth hanging open. "Jumping jackrabbits! Tara, whatever you're doing, keep doing it!" he shouted, his voice filled with a mix of panic and awe.

Andy's jaw dropped, and for once, he was utterly speechless. He stared at the feather, blinking rapidly. "Incredible!" he gasped. "It's not just light—it's pure magic! The kind that legends are made of!"

Tara held the feather high, feeling the warmth of its light flow through her like a heartbeat, steady and strong. She wasn't just holding a feather—she was holding hope itself. The light seemed to fill her, pushing back the fear, the doubt, the darkness that had threatened to swallow her whole.

"Shade!" Tara shouted, her voice no longer trembling. It was steady, powerful. "You can't stop us! This light—it's stronger than your shadows, stronger than any fear you throw at us! We're not turning back!"

The feather's light grew even brighter, spreading out like a shield, driving the shadows back farther and farther. Shade shrieked in fury, its form breaking apart like smoke caught in a storm.

"This isn't over!" it howled, its voice laced with rage and desperation. "You think this light will save you? You think you can defeat Lord Nightweaver? He'll crush you! He'll—"

But before it could finish, the light exploded in one final burst, sending Shade hurtling back into the darkness, its shape dissolving into the air. The oppressive chill lifted, the forest breathing back to life with colors and warmth. The flowers straightened, their vibrant hues returning, and the sun broke through the canopy, lighting up the leaves like green glass.

Tara lowered the feather, her hands shaking not from fear but from the sheer force of the moment. She looked at Toby and Andy, her friends who had stood with her through it all.

Toby was grinning again, his legs wobbly but full of energy. "Now that's what I call turning the tide!" he said, giving a shaky fist pump. "Who knew you had that kind of firepower in you, Tara?"

Andy adjusted his goggles, his eyes practically popping with curiosity. "Incredible! That's a feather from a Lumina Bird! I thought they were just legends! They're said to be guardians of light, protectors against the darkest of magic."

Tara gently tucked the feather back into her pack, her mind swirling with questions. Who had left her this powerful gift? And how did Shade know exactly who she was?

"Well," Toby said, glancing nervously at the shadows, "I think it's safe to say we've got a big target on our backs now. Let's keep moving before Mr. Creepy-Crawly decides to bring some friends."

Tara nodded, the fear in her chest now mixed with a burning determination. "You're right, Toby. We need to get to the Whispering Willow fast. There's more at stake here than I ever imagined."

As they continued deeper into the forest, the encounter with Shade hung over them like a cloud. But something had changed. They were no longer just three creatures walking separate paths—they were a team now, bound together by a purpose bigger than any one of them.

Unbeknownst to them, deep within the Crystal Caves, Lord Nightweaver was already planning his next move. The darkness was spreading, and he would stop at nothing to see Taranterra fall.

But for now, as Tara, Toby, and Andy pressed on through the sun-dappled paths of the Whispering Forest, hope was alive.

In a place like Taranterra, where magic was as real as the trees and the stars, even the smallest creatures could change the fate of an entire kingdom.

The Whispering Willow awaited them, and with it, the next step in Tara's journey. What secrets would it hold? What challenges lay ahead? One thing was clear—this was only the beginning of the greatest adventure Taranterra had ever seen.

CHAPTER 3

SECRETS OF THE WHISPERING WILLOW

As Tara, Toby, and Andy reached the Whispering Willow, the whole forest seemed to grow quiet. The encounter with Shade was still fresh in their minds, leaving them shaken but even more determined. The great tree stood tall and twisted, its ancient branches swaying slightly in a breeze that didn't seem to come from anywhere.

"Well, this is it," Toby said, bouncing nervously on his legs. "The Whispering Willow! Though, I have to say, it's not exactly whispering. More like... mumbling?"

Andy adjusted the straps on his goggles, glancing up at the ancient tree. "Maybe it's just shy. Not every tree wakes up chatty. But don't worry, folks—lucky for you, I have just the thing!"

Before anyone could respond, Andy pulled out a strange contraption from his bag. It looked like a mishmash of tubes, gears, and a funnel stuck together with glowing threads of silk. "Presenting the Tree Translator 2000! Patented, experimental, and prone to minor—" he gave Tara a quick glance, "—okay, occasional explosive side effects."

SECRETS OF THE WHISPERING WILLOW

Toby gave him a deadpan stare. "Yeah, because the one thing this delicate moment needs is an explosion."

Andy grinned. "Relax. This beauty's been fine-tuned to... probably not blow up." He pressed a button, and the device whirred to life, sending little sparks of light through the tubes. He held the funnel up to the bark. "Go ahead, Big Guy. Tell us your secrets."

The tree remained perfectly still.

"Okay," Toby said, leaning closer with a smirk. "Let the professional handle this." He cleared his throat dramatically. "What's a tree's favorite drink?"

Andy groaned. "Don't."

Toby gave a sly grin. "Root beer."

The Willow remained silent.

"Okay, okay. Tough crowd," Toby muttered. He tapped the bark lightly with one of his legs. "How about this—what did the tree say to the lumberjack? 'I'm rooting for you.' Get it?"

Tara covered her mouth, trying not to laugh. "Toby, you're going to make it mad."

"Trees love jokes!" Toby protested, puffing up. "I'm building rapport."

Andy crossed his legs, holding back a grin. "Yeah, if by rapport you mean cringe. What's your next plan, telling it to leaf you alone?"

Toby gave him a playful nudge. "Hey, at least I'm trying. What's your backup plan, genius?"

Andy held the funnel back up to the tree, tapping it lightly. "Listen, Willow, buddy. I know waking up after a few centuries must be rough—roots stiff, bark cracking, all that. But work with us here. No explosions, I promise. Just a little conversation?"

The Willow gave no response.

"Maybe it's on tree time?" Andy suggested, turning to Tara. "You know, super slow and dramatic."

Toby leaned in toward the bark again. "Alright, how about this one—why don't trees play poker? Because they always fold." He turned back to Andy with a smug grin. "Boom. That's gold."

Andy clapped his legs together in mock applause. "Wow. That joke was timber-rific. Truly, a masterpiece."

Just as Toby was about to fire off another one-liner, the Willow's bark groaned deeply, sending a shiver through the air. Slowly, its twisted trunk began to shift, the ancient wood creaking as if it hadn't moved in centuries. The bark curled and bent, revealing the outline of a weathered, wise face within the tree, eyes half-lidded with the weight of ages.

Both Toby and Andy immediately stopped their antics, standing frozen as if they had accidentally summoned an ancient storm.

The Willow's eyes opened fully, glowing faintly with soft, green light. Its voice rumbled like distant thunder, low and calm, but with a gravity that made the air feel heavier.

"Ah, young travelers," it said, the sound like wind rustling through forgotten leaves. "And the lost princess, returned at last. You've been quite noisy, haven't you?"

Toby gave a nervous chuckle, rubbing the back of his head. "Well, you know... Just trying to lighten the mood. Didn't mean to bark up the wrong tree."

Tara shot him a look. "Seriously, Toby?"

Andy elbowed Toby lightly, barely holding in a laugh. "Let the tree talk, hero."

The Willow's expression shifted into something that might have been amusement—or maybe just pity. "We have waited for many years, Princess Tara," it said slowly. "Time is woven into every root and branch of this island, and you are the thread that must stitch it back together."

Tara's heart skipped a beat. The Willow's words felt heavy with meaning, settling over her like a cloak she hadn't realized she'd been wearing all along.

"Wait, hold up," Toby whispered to Andy, though not quietly enough. "Did that tree just call her the thread? That sounds... serious."

Andy gave a mock whisper back. "Yeah, no kidding. Guess we're in the high-stakes prophecy department now."

The Willow's ancient gaze fell on Tara again, ignoring their chit-chat. "You are more than what you know, child. The path ahead will demand courage, wisdom, and compassion. But the answers lie not in the trials alone—they lie within you."

Tara swallowed hard, her legs trembling slightly. "So... it's true?" she whispered, her voice barely audible. "I really am the lost princess?"

The Willow's branches swayed, almost like it was nodding. "Indeed, you are, child. But more than a princess, you are the hope of Taranterra. A great darkness looms over our land—the Shadow Weavers have returned."

Andy's eyes widened, his wings giving a nervous flutter. "Shadow Weavers? But those are just bedtime stories, right? The kind you tell to make little bugs behave?"

The Willow's expression turned serious. "I'm afraid they are no legend, young one. The Shadow Weavers were defeated long ago by your parents, Tara, but now they are back, ready to drown Taranterra in darkness. Only you can stop them."

Tara's head spun. How could she possibly face a threat like that? As if sensing her doubt, the Willow gently reached out one of its branches and brushed Tara's cheek.

"Do not fear," the Willow whispered. "You are not alone. The Silk of Destiny has chosen three guardians to stand by your side."

With that, the ground beneath the tree shifted, and its roots parted to reveal a hidden chamber. Inside, glowing softly, were three magical items: a shimmering cloak, a compass that seemed to shine like a star, and a delicate silver flute.

"The Cloak of Shadows will hide you from sight," the Willow explained. "The Starlight Compass will guide your way, and the Whisperwind Flute will call for help when you need it most. These will aid you in your quest, Princess Tara."

Tara picked up the magical items with trembling hands, her eyes full of determination and doubt. "I don't know if I'm ready for this," she admitted, her voice barely more than a whisper.

Toby placed a hand on her shoulder, giving her a lopsided grin. "Ready or not, we've got your back, Princess. And besides, what's the worst that could happen, right? Oh wait, don't answer that."

Andy adjusted his goggles, nodding seriously. "Together, we'll make sure the darkness doesn't stand a chance."

Just as Tara was about to say something, the ground shook beneath their feet. The Whispering Willow's leaves rustled violently, and its bark-etched face showed a look of alarm.

"Quickly!" the Willow cried, its voice urgent. "The Shadow Weavers are near! You must hide!"

Without thinking, Tara threw the Cloak of Shadows over herself and her friends. The cloak seemed to wrap them in darkness, hiding them from sight just in time. A second later, a group of shadowy figures glided into the clearing, their eyes glowing like coals in the night.

"I can smell them, brothers," one of the Shadow Weavers hissed, its voice like nails on glass. "The princess and her little friends were here. Find them!"

The forest pulsed with tension as Tara, Toby, and Andy held their breath, inching backward one careful step at a time. The night clung to them, thick and silent, as if the forest itself was holding its breath.

And then—

SNAP!

Toby's foot caught on a root, and he tumbled into the bushes with a yelp.

Every Shadow Weaver's head jerked toward the noise, their glowing green eyes locking onto the trio like hungry predators.

"There!" one hissed, its twisted leg pointing straight at them. "After them!"

"RUN!" Tara shouted, yanking Toby upright.

They tore into the forest like a shot, leaves and branches whipping past as they sprinted through the dense woods. The sound of scuttling legs and cold, eerie laughter echoed behind them, sharp and close, like thousands of whispers crawling along their spines.

"This way!" Andy panted, spotting a narrow crack between two jagged boulders. "Through here—NOW!"

Without thinking, they dove through the gap, scraping legs and bodies against the rough stone. Toby let out a muttered curse as he nearly tripped again, and Andy grumbled, "Toby, you fall one more time, and I'm leaving you behind."

"I'm built for charm, not speed!" Toby snapped, scrambling after them.

They tumbled out the other side, landing hard on their legs. What lay before them was nothing short of surreal—a forest of glowing mushrooms, their enormous caps glowing in shades of green, blue, and violet.

"The Fungal Forest," Toby whispered, awestruck. "It's real!"

"Yeah, yeah, it's real—keep moving!" Tara hissed, pulling him along.

The forest held its breath as Tara, Toby, and Andy crouched low, their hearts hammering like drums in their chests. Every sound seemed amplified—the crunch of leaves underfoot, the rustle of branches in the wind. They moved slowly, inch by inch, hoping the darkness would hide them.

Then it happened. Toby's back leg caught on a gnarly root.

"Whoa—!" he yelped, tumbling forward with a graceless thud into the bushes.

The snap of twigs echoed like a firecracker in the stillness.

The Shadow Weavers' heads twisted in unison, their glowing green eyes locking onto the noise. "There!" one of them hissed, its voice like the scrape of nails on stone. "Get them!"

Tara didn't wait. She grabbed Toby's leg and hauled him to his feet. "Run!" she shouted, sprinting toward the dense forest ahead.

"Go, go, go!" Andy yelled, his legs scrambling beneath him as if they'd taken on a mind of their own.

The Shadow Weavers surged after them, moving like waves of dark smoke, their cold laughter trailing behind—sharp and sinister, a hundred voices whispering at once.

Branches clawed at their fur, thorns scraped their legs, and roots snaked up to trip them as they raced deeper into the forest. Tara could feel the Shadow Weavers closing the gap, their twisted forms gliding over the ground, faster than seemed possible.

"This is bad. This is really bad!" Toby gasped, dodging a low-hanging branch that nearly took his head off.

"Thanks for the update!" Tara snapped, ducking under a tangle of vines.

Andy sprinted beside them, his goggles bouncing on his head. "We're not dying today!" he hollered. "If anyone's going to explode, it's going to be on my terms!"

Through the chaos, Andy spotted a narrow gap between two enormous rocks ahead. "This way!" he shouted, pointing toward it. "It's tight, but it might slow them down!"

They squeezed through the gap, the rough stone scraping their sides. Behind them, the Shadow Weavers hissed, their smoky bodies struggling to squeeze through the narrow crack.

On the other side, the forest suddenly gave way to an astonishing sight—the Fungal Forest. Towering mushrooms glowed softly in hues of green, blue, and purple, their caps shimmering like lanterns in the dim light.

"The Fungal Forest?" Toby panted, eyes wide. "I thought this place was a bedtime story!"

Tara yanked him along. "Myths or not, run!"

The Shadow Weavers twisted through the rock gap behind them, their smoky limbs reforming, slithering after them with terrifying speed.

Andy glanced over his shoulder and gulped. "Uh, we're fresh out of hiding spots!"

Without slowing down, Tara spotted the tallest mushroom ahead—a giant with a thick stalk that reached the canopy above. "Up there!" she called, pointing.

"Climbing?! Great idea, love it!" Toby wheezed sarcastically. "Because we all know how much I love heights!"

But with the Shadow Weavers just a few feet behind, they didn't have a choice. Using strands of silk, the three spiders shot upward, scaling the mushroom stalk in a desperate scramble. The stalk swayed slightly under their weight, but they didn't stop until they were tucked beneath the mushroom's glowing cap, gasping for breath.

Tara fumbled with the Starlight Compass, her hands shaking. The needle spun wildly for a moment, as if unsure which way to point, then locked in a direction toward the distant peaks. "The Glimmering Mountains," she whispered, "that's where we need to go."

Andy peeked down over the edge. "Yeah, cool. But, uh... how do we get there without becoming villain-spider snacks?"

Below, the Shadow Weavers gathered at the base of the mushroom, their twisted legs scraping against the stalk, preparing to climb.

Toby groaned, his voice low and panicked. "Anyone else feel like we just volunteered to be appetizers?"

"Over here!"

They turned toward the sound and saw a tiny glowing sprite hovering on the edge of the mushroom cap. Her wings shimmered with a soft, silver glow, like moonlight captured in flight.

"I'm Luminara, Guardian of the Fungal Forest!" she whispered urgently. "If you want to survive, you have to jump!"

"Jump?" Toby's voice cracked. "As in, off this giant mushroom? Are you out of your mind?"

"Do it, or get eaten. Your choice!" Luminara called, her glow intensifying. "The caps will carry you across the forest—if you trust them."

Tara didn't hesitate. "We trust you!"

She leaped first, springing off the mushroom cap. It bent slightly under her weight, then snapped back like a slingshot, launching her into the air.

"Whoa!" Tara shouted, soaring through the forest. She landed on another mushroom with a soft bounce, barely sticking the landing.

Toby's legs shook as he stared down. "This is nuts. This is completely nuts!"

Andy gave him a cheeky nudge. "Then what are you waiting for, Mr. Hero? Jump!"

With a loud groan, Toby launched himself off the cap. "I'm going to regret this!" he yelled as he flew through the air—and landed with a solid bounce on the next mushroom.

Andy followed, laughing as he tumbled through the air. "I never thought bouncing would be a survival skill!"

The Shadow Weavers hissed below, their dark forms trying to claw their way up the mushroom stalk. But Tara, Toby, and Andy were already leaping from cap to cap, soaring through the glowing forest like daredevils.

"This is crazy!" Toby shouted, a grin splitting his face despite the fear. "I love it!"

Andy landed next to him, legs wobbling. "If we survive this, I'm adding 'Mushroom Acrobat' to my resume!"

The Shadow Weavers tried to follow, but their smoky forms struggled to grip the slippery mushrooms. Frustrated hisses filled the air as Tara and her friends sailed further and further away.

"Almost there!" Tara called, spotting the edge of the Fungal Forest just ahead.

With one final leap, they launched themselves off the last mushroom and tumbled onto solid ground, landing in a heap of tangled legs and laughter.

Toby groaned, flat on his back. "Next time, you explain to the mushrooms what we're doing."

Luminara fluttered beside them, glowing brighter than ever. "You did it! I told you the mushrooms would carry you."

Andy adjusted his goggles, still catching his breath. "Remind me to never doubt glowing sprites again."

As they stood, the forest behind them darkened, the Shadow Weavers hissing in frustration as they vanished back into the shadows.

Tara dusted herself off, her eyes now locked on the distant peaks of the Glimmering Mountains.

"No more detours," she said, her voice steady. "We head to the Crystal Caves—and we don't stop until we reach them."

Toby gave a weak thumbs-up from the ground. "Yeah, yeah. Just... give me five minutes to remember how to walk again."

Andy patted him on the back with a grin. "C'mon, hero. No rest for the brave."

And with that, the trio gathered themselves, ready for the next leg of their journey, the thrill of the chase still pulsing through their veins.

CHAPTER 4

PERILS OF THE CRYSTAL CAVES

Tara, Toby, and Andy stood at the base of the Glimmering Mountains, staring up at the Crystal Caves. The entrance shimmered in a dance of light and color, almost like the cave itself was alive, breathing with hidden energy.

"Wow," Toby said, his mouth open wide, "this place looks like it's wearing a million diamond necklaces!"

"Imagine the scientific discoveries we could make here!" Andy added, his wings buzzing with excitement. "I mean, just think of the crystals! The way they glow—it could power my inventions for years!"

Tara forced a smile at their excitement, but inside, her nerves were tight. She couldn't shake the words of the Whispering Willow from her mind: great dangers lie ahead. She took a deep breath, steadying herself. "We've come this far," she said. "Let's see what the Crystal Caves have in store for us."

As they approached the cave entrance, they felt a sudden pulse of energy, like an invisible barrier blocking their

PERILS OF THE CRYSTAL CAVES

way. The air around them seemed to hum, and a strange symbol glowed on the cave's mouth—a mark they couldn't understand.

"What's that supposed to mean?" Toby asked, scratching his head. "Looks like the cave's put up a 'No Trespassing' sign."

Andy adjusted his goggles and squinted at the symbol. "It's some kind of spell," he said thoughtfully. "A lock, of sorts. We need to break it if we're going to get inside."

Just then, words began to carve themselves into the rock face, glowing with a soft blue light. The letters twisted and shifted, forming a riddle more puzzling than any they had seen before:

"I bloom in silence, hidden by night,
A secret kept from the sun's first light.
Find me where shadows dare not tread,
My petals glow where light is fed.
In the grasp of thorns, my heart does stay,
Bring me forth, and clear the way."

"A riddle!" Tara said, her brow furrowed in concentration. "We need to figure this out to break the spell."

"Whoa, that's a tricky one," Toby muttered, rubbing his temples. "Something about a flower that hides in the dark and glows in the light... but where shadows dare not tread? And what's this about thorns?"

Andy's eyes went wide with realization. "I've got it!" he said, nearly jumping out of his skin. "It's the Dawnpetal! It's a rare flower that only blooms in the first light of day and hides itself when darkness falls. But it's protected by a thorny guardian—a magical creature that won't let anyone near it."

Tara's heart skipped a beat. "So it's not just finding the flower, it's getting past the creature that guards it. Great," she said, her voice filled with both determination and a hint of dread.

Toby sighed dramatically. "Oh, perfect. Not only do we have to solve a riddle, but now we've got to face some spiky monster, too? Just another day in the life of a princess and her loyal sidekick, I guess!"

Tara pulled out the Starlight Compass, hoping it would guide them. The needle spun wildly before pointing toward a narrow, overgrown path that wound around the mountainside. "This way," she said, gripping the compass tightly. "Let's find that flower."

They followed the path, which seemed to get darker and narrower the further they went. Every step felt like a challenge, with rocks shifting under their feet and the air growing colder. Suddenly, they entered a small clearing bathed in a strange light, almost like the sun itself was trapped in this hidden place.

There, in the center of the clearing, stood the Dawnpetal—a single, radiant flower glowing with soft golden light. But it wasn't alone. Circling the flower, eyes narrowed and glowing a fierce emerald green, was a creature unlike any they had ever seen. It was a Thornbeast, a massive feline-like creature covered in twisting vines and sharp thorns. Its growl rumbled low and deep, echoing in the clearing like a warning.

"That's the guardian," Andy whispered, his voice shaking. "A Thornbeast. It protects the Dawnpetal with everything it's got."

Toby gulped loudly. "Okay, so...anyone have a plan that doesn't involve getting shredded into spider confetti?"

Tara thought quickly, her mind racing. "The riddle said the flower glows where light is fed and hides in the dark. What if we can distract the Thornbeast long enough to get the flower?"

Andy's eyes lit up. "Brilliant! If we use the Whisperwind Flute, we might be able to create a light that attracts its attention away from the Dawnpetal!"

Tara nodded and pulled out the Whisperwind Flute from her pack. She took a deep breath and played a soft, haunting melody. The sound filled the air, and to their amazement, tiny sparks of light began to dance around the clearing, like fireflies made of stardust. The Thornbeast's eyes followed the lights, its growl softening as it became mesmerized by the glowing shapes.

"Now!" Tara whispered urgently. "While it's distracted!"

Toby crept forward on tiptoes, moving like he was sneaking cookies from the pantry. He reached out and gently plucked the Dawnpetal, careful not to damage its delicate petals. The moment he had it in his hands, the flower's glow intensified, and the magical barrier on the cave's entrance flickered and began to dissolve.

"We did it!" Toby whispered, holding up the flower like a trophy.

But just then, the Thornbeast snapped out of its trance, its eyes blazing with anger. It let out a roar that shook the ground beneath them. "Uh, Tara?" Toby said, backing away slowly. "I think our distraction just wore off!"

Andy grabbed the Starlight Compass, his voice shaking with urgency. "Run! Back to the cave entrance—now!"

They reached the cave entrance, the barrier flickering as Tara crushed the delicate petals of the Dawnpetal in her hands. The glowing dust scattered over the enchanted symbol etched into the stone. With a blinding flash, the barrier shattered, the air humming with released magic as the Thornbeast screeched to a halt, unable to cross the threshold.

"We made it!" Tara gasped, her legs shaking with exhaustion.

But before she could catch her breath, a low hiss echoed behind them. One of the Thornbeast's thorny tendrils shot out, lashing around Toby's leg and yanking him off his feet.

"Ahh! Help!" Toby shouted, his legs flailing as he was dragged back toward the furious creature.

"Toby!" Tara screamed, scrambling toward him. But the Thornbeast snarled, dragging Toby further away, its emerald eyes blazing with rage.

Andy fumbled with the Whisperwind Flute, but his hands shook too badly to play. "Tara, do something!" he cried.

Tara tried to move, but fear pinned her in place—until, out of nowhere, a voice boomed through the air like the crack of a whip.

"Not today, beast!"

A familiar figure shot out of the shadows—Captain Silkbeard, her silver beard gleaming in the dim light as he lunged toward the Thornbeast without hesitation.

"Captain!" Tara gasped.

Silkbeard's movements were fluid and fierce, her eight legs spinning silk faster than the eye could follow, tangling the Thornbeast's limbs as it roared in fury.

"Get him out of here!" Silkbeard shouted, dodging the Thornbeast's snapping jaws. "Now!"

Without thinking, Tara and Andy rushed toward Toby, grabbing him by his legs and pulling him free from the beast's thorny grasp.

"Go! Get inside the cave!" Silkbeard barked, circling the beast like a storm. Her voice held no fear, only the steady command of someone who knew his fate—and had accepted it.

"No, Captain! Come with us!" Tara begged, her voice cracking with desperation.

But Silkbeard smiled, a calm, knowing smile, as she spun a final thread to bind the Thornbeast's legs. "This fight's mine, little one. You have your own battles to win."

The Thornbeast roared, thrashing wildly, tearing through the silk bindings. But Silkbeard held her ground, blocking the path between the beast and the young spiders.

"Go!" she shouted one last time, and with heavy hearts, Tara, Toby, and Andy stumbled back through the entrance of the cave.

As they crossed the threshold, the magical barrier shimmered to life again, sealing them inside. From the other side, they saw Captain Silkbeard standing tall, facing the enraged Thornbeast head-on.

The Thornbeast lunged, and Silkbeard met it with everything she had—legs moving in a blur, silk flying like streaks of silver in the night. For a moment, it looked as though she might win.

Then the beast struck. A thorny tendril slashed through the air, piercing through Silkbeard's side.

"Captain!" Tara screamed, banging on the barrier as if sheer willpower could break it.

Silkbeard staggered, her legs trembling under him, but she kept fighting, spinning silk with one last burst of strength. The Thornbeast growled low, wrapping him in its thorny vines. But even as it pulled her close, Silkbeard smiled through the pain.

"Remember, Tara," she whispered, though his voice was barely audible through the barrier. "A captain always sails toward the storm... not away from it."

And then the Thornbeast struck one final time. With a terrible roar, it dragged Silkbeard down, wrapping her in shadows and thorns.

Tara slammed her legs against the barrier, tears blurring her vision. "No! No, Captain!"

Andy pulled her back gently but urgently. "We can't help him now, Tara. He gave us a chance—we have to keep going."

Toby, still catching his breath, placed a shaky leg on Tara's shoulder. "We have to make it worth it, Tara. For him."

Through her tears, Tara nodded, her heart breaking under the weight of the loss. Captain Silkbeard had saved them, sacrificing himself so they could continue their quest. And now it was up to them to make sure his sacrifice wasn't in vain.

With one last, heart-wrenching look at the fading figure of Silkbeard, Tara whispered, "I'll finish this. I promise."

They turned away from the barrier, their hearts heavy but their resolve stronger than ever. As they moved deeper into the cave, the echoes of Silkbeard's last words seemed to follow them, a reminder of the courage it takes to face the storm—and the sacrifice that sometimes comes with it.

And though Captain Silkbeard was gone, her spirit sailed on, carried in the hearts of those he saved, guiding them toward the light in the darkest moments of their journey.

Tara, still holding the remnants of the Dawnpetal, looked deeper into the dark tunnel of the cave. Her face was a mix of fear and determination. "We're not just solving puzzles anymore," she said quietly. "We're fighting for Taranterra. And this is just the beginning."

They took a moment to steady themselves, and with the cave's dark path opening before them, they stepped into the unknown, ready for whatever dangers and discoveries awaited them next.

Tara, Toby, and Andy entered the Crystal Caves, the darkness swallowing them whole. The air was cool and damp, every step echoing off the shimmering walls. Crystals jutted out from every surface, casting eerie reflections that seemed to watch them as they moved.

"Alright, team," Tara said, her voice a little shaky but firm, "let's stick together. No wandering off."

"Trust me, I'm not going anywhere on my own in this spooky place," Toby said, eyes darting around nervously. "I'm sticking to you like glue!"

As they ventured deeper, the magical items from the Whispering Willow proved their worth. The Starlight Compass led them through the twisting tunnels, its needle steady and true, guiding them when the paths seemed to shift and change. The Cloak of Shadows helped them slip past strange creatures that glowed in the darkness, their eyes like tiny lanterns flickering in the cave's depths.

But then, without warning, Andy's Lumin-Essence Detector started beeping wildly, its lights flashing red. "Oh dear," Andy stammered, his antennae twitching nervously. "We've got trouble—an enormous surge of dark energy just ahead!"

Before anyone could react, the ground began to rumble. The crystals in the cave walls vibrated, and cracks spread across the floor like spider webs. Dark, shadowy tendril shot up from the cracks, writhing like snakes, reaching for them with an evil intent.

"Look out!" Tara shouted, diving out of the way as a tendril lashed toward her, missing by inches. "It's the Shadow Weavers' magic!"

Toby leapt into action, his movements swift and agile. "Follow me!" he yelled, hopping from crystal to crystal, dodging the shadowy tentacles with the grace of a cat. "I see a way out of this mess!"

Tara and Andy followed as best they could, but just when they thought they might escape, a thick tendril lashed out, wrapping itself around Andy's legs. The Smart inventor was yanked off his feet, pulled toward a deep, dark chasm that seemed to have no end.

"Tara!" Andy cried out, his voice filled with panic as he struggled against the pull. "Help!"

Without thinking, Tara grabbed the Whisperwind Flute from her pack. She blew into it, and a clear, pure note rang through the caves. The sound echoed off the walls, like a beacon cutting through the darkness. Suddenly, a swarm of bioluminescent fireflies burst into the air, their tiny bodies glowing like stars. They surrounded Andy, their light so bright that the tendril recoiled in pain, letting go of its grip.

Andy tumbled to the ground, gasping for breath but safe. "I owe you one, Tara," he said, his eyes wide with relief. "I thought I was done for!"

"You'd better stick with us, Andy," Toby said with a grin, pulling the moth to his feet. "We've got a lot more of these shadowy tricks to get through."

They moved quickly, weaving through the remaining tendrils until they finally reached a massive domed chamber at the heart of the caves. At its center stood a portal, swirling with an eerie purple light that pulsed like a heartbeat.

"The entrance to the Shadow Weavers' realm,"Tara said, her voice barely more than a whisper. The sight of the portal sent a chill down her spine.

Before they could get any closer, a cold, cruel laugh echoed through the chamber. The shadows seemed to pull together, forming a tall, dark figure. Out of the darkness stepped Lord Nightweaver, his eyes glowing with a malevolent light.

"Welcome, little princess," he sneered, his voice dripping with mockery. "I am Lord Nightweaver, master of the Shadow Weavers. We've been expecting you."

Tara's knees felt weak, but she forced herself to stand tall, meeting his gaze with a courage she wasn't sure she truly felt. "Your reign of darkness ends here, Nightweaver," she said, her voice steady. "We won't let you destroy Taranterra!"

Nightweaver's laughter grew louder, colder. "Oh, how delightful!" he said. "You think you can stand against me? Foolish girl, you have no idea of the power you face. Taranterra will fall, and you will watch as your precious kingdom is swallowed by eternal night!"

With a swift movement, Nightweaver waved his leg, and a horde of shadow creatures rose from the ground, their eyes glowing with hunger, their forms shifting like black smoke ready to devour everything in their path.

Just as the shadow creatures lunged toward them, a brilliant light filled the chamber. The darkness seemed to crack and pull back, and from a hidden alcove stepped a magnificent

Lumina Bird. Its feathers shimmered with all the colors of the rainbow, glowing brighter than the sun itself.

"Halt, Nightweaver!" the Lumina Bird commanded, its voice like music that echoed through the cave. "You forget the ancient laws. The princess must be given a chance to prove herself worthy."

Nightweaver hissed in frustration, his eyes narrowing into slits. "Very well," he growled. "The Three Trials of Taranterra, then. If you survive, little princess, we shall see who truly deserves to rule this realm."

With a sweep of its radiant wings, the Lumina Bird transformed the chamber. Three doorways appeared in the walls of the cave, each one glowing with a different light—The Golden Veil of Valor, The Silver Gate of Secrets, and The Bronze Passage of Trials.

"Choose wisely, Princess Tara," the Lumina Bird said, its eyes steady on her. "Each door leads to a trial that will test your courage, wisdom, and compassion. But remember—you may only take one companion with you into each trial."

Tara turned to her friends, her mind racing. She had to choose carefully. "Toby," she said, looking at her loyal friend, "your quick thinking and speed will be essential. You'll come with me for the first trial."

Toby's face broke into a wide grin, bouncing on his feet. "You got it, Tara! Let's show these shadow creeps what we're made of!"

Tara then looked at Andy. "Your knowledge and inventions could be the key to the second trial," she said, her voice filled with trust.

Andy nodded, his antennae buzzing with determination. "Consider me at your service, Princess. We'll crack that trial wide open!"

Finally, Tara faced the Lumina Bird. "For the third trial, if it's allowed," she said, her voice soft but sure, "I want you by my side. I have a feeling your light will be the only thing strong enough to fight the darkness."

The Lumina Bird bowed its head in agreement, its feathers glowing even brighter. "A wise choice, young one," it said.

With hearts pounding and adrenaline rushing through their veins, Tara and Toby stepped through the The Golden Veil of Valor. They had no idea what awaited them on the other side, but they knew one thing for sure—they were ready to face whatever challenge the shadows had in store. This was their moment to prove themselves and to fight for Taranterra.

Tara and Toby stepped through the The Golden Veil of Valor and found themselves in a vast crystal cave. The walls shimmered and glinted, constantly shifting, like they were alive, twisting into new shapes every second. In the center of it all, floating over a bottomless chasm, hung a glowing key, its light pulsing like a heartbeat.

"That's it," Tara said, pointing to the key. "We need that to pass the trial. But how in the world do we reach it?"

No sooner had she spoken than the labyrinth began to move, the walls sliding and rearranging at a dizzying speed. From the corners of the maze, figures emerged—creatures made of living crystal, their bodies faceted and sharp, reflecting light like a thousand tiny mirrors. They moved toward them, each step ringing out like glass shattering.

"Holy mother of spiders" Toby shouted, his eyes wide with panic. "I don't suppose you have a plan, Tara?"

Tara's mind raced. They needed to get that key, but those crystal creatures were closing in fast. Then, an idea struck her like lightning. "The Cloak of Shadows!" she said. "Toby, if you wear it, you can slip past them without being seen and reach the key!"

"Are you sure?" Toby asked, grabbing the cloak. "What about you?"

"I'll use the Starlight Compass to lead these creatures away from you," Tara replied, her voice calm but urgent. "I'll draw their attention while you go for the key. We don't have much time—go!"

Toby nodded, a determined look on his face. He threw the Cloak of Shadows over his shoulders, and just like that, he seemed to vanish, blending into the shifting light of the labyrinth. Tara held up the Starlight Compass, its glow steady, guiding her through the maze. She took a deep breath and charged forward, leading the crystal creatures on a wild chase.

"Hey, shiny faces! Over here!" she called, waving her arms to get their attention. The creatures hissed and turned their jagged heads toward her, their movements becoming more frantic as they followed the glow of the compass.

Meanwhile, Toby, hidden by the Cloak of Shadows, darted between the crystal walls, his movements quick and silent. He leapt from one ledge to another, his eyes locked on the glowing key. The maze kept shifting, walls closing in and passages disappearing, but he was fast, faster than he'd ever been.

The creatures kept closing in on Tara, their bodies clinking and clattering as they moved. "Come on, come on!" she muttered under her breath, guiding them further away from Toby. Sweat dripped down her face, but she didn't let up. The compass led her through twists and turns, keeping her just one step ahead.

Toby saw his moment. With the last bit of strength, he leapt toward the glowing key, his legs stretched out as far as they could go. He reached out, fingers trembling, and just as the maze seemed ready to shift again, his hands wrapped around the key.

The instant Toby touched the key, the entire labyrinth froze. The crystal creatures shattered into pieces, their bodies breaking apart into harmless shards that fell to the floor like rain. The ground stopped shaking, and a doorway of light appeared at the end of the chamber.

"We did it!" Tara cried out, running to Toby and pulling him into a tight hug. "You got the key!"

Toby grinned, panting heavily. "All in a day's work! Although, next time, let's pick a trial that doesn't involve shiny monsters trying to squish us, alright?"

They stepped through the doorway and found themselves back in the central chamber, where Andy and the Lumina Bird were waiting anxiously. The relief on their faces was clear as soon as they saw their friends return safely.

"One trial down," the Lumina Bird said, its voice calm and filled with approval. "But two more remain, each more challenging than the last. Are you ready to continue, brave ones?"

Tara looked at her friends, seeing the same determination in their eyes that burned in her own. "We're ready," she said firmly. "For Taranterra!"

As they turned toward the The Silver Gate of Secrets, a shadow shifted in the corner of the chamber. Unnoticed by any of them, Shade, Nightweaver's twisted servant, watched with a smirk. He slipped silently back into the darkness, ready to report to his master.

The fight for Taranterra was far from over. But in that moment, as Tara, Toby, Andy, and the Lumina Bird prepared for the next trial, they knew that whatever awaited them, they would face it together.

With their courage unbroken and their bond stronger than ever, they stepped toward the The Silver Gate of Secrets, ready to dive headfirst into the next challenge, knowing that the fate of their world rested in their hands.

CHAPTER 5

SHADOWS AND LIGHT

Tara turned to Andy, determination burning in her eyes. "Andy, are you ready for the next trial?" she asked.

Andy replied in excitement "Ready as ever, Princess! My Lumin-Essence Detector is fine-tuned and ready to light up the dark!"

Tara gave him a quick nod, her hand steady as she reached for the The Silver Gate of Secrets. Together, she and Andy stepped through, the world around them shimmering and warping like a reflection in a pond.

When the world settled, they found themselves in a massive chamber filled with whirring gears, swinging pendulums, and twisting clockwork mechanisms. The place was alive with movement, like a giant puzzle in constant motion.

"Holy mother of spiders!" Andy gasped, eyes wide. "It's the Timesphere! This is where Taranterra's time is kept in balance!"

But something was terribly wrong. The gears were grinding loudly, the pendulums swinging wildly out of sync, and

SHADOWS AND LIGHT

at the center stood a massive hourglass, its glass cracked, leaking sand onto the floor.

A deep, echoing voice filled the chamber. "Time is unraveling in Taranterra. Mend the Timesphere, or all will be lost to chaos!"

Andy's eyes narrowed in determination. "Right, no time to waste," he said, pulling out a toolkit from his pack. "We've got to fix this mess before the whole thing collapses on itself!"

Tara and Andy jumped into action, darting from one broken gear to another. Andy's hands moved like lightning, using his inventions to reset gears that had rusted to nothing in seconds. Tara used the Starlight Compass to guide them through the maze of machinery, the needle pointing to the most critical parts that needed their attention.

"Over there!" Andy shouted, his voice strained with focus. "That gear's aging a century every second! If we don't stabilize it, we'll lose all control of the clockwork!"

Tara rushed to the gear, her hands shaking as she reached out to steady it. Just then, she caught a glimpse of something in the polished metal—her own reflection, but older, wiser, with a crown on her head. Her future self looked at her with a knowing smile and said softly, "Remember, Tara, the key lies in the balance between what was, what is, and what could be."

The words sent a chill down Tara's spine, but they also filled her with a strange sense of calm. She knew what to do. "Andy, slow it down just a little," she said. "It's not just about fixing the present—we have to balance it with the past and future."

Andy nodded, his hands moving with more purpose now, recalibrating the gears to turn in harmony. Tara adjusted the pendulums so they swung evenly, their rhythm no longer pulling the past and future apart.

As they worked, images flickered around them—visions of Taranterra's past, scenes of its founding, and possible futures where shadows covered the land. But there were also glimpses of a brighter tomorrow, where light and shadow lived in balance, where all creatures worked together to keep the harmony.

With one final turn of a gear, the giant hourglass in the center of the chamber began to mend itself. Cracks sealed up, and the sand inside flowed smoothly once more, marking time as it should. The grinding noise faded into a gentle ticking, and the room fell still.

"We did it!" Tara cried, throwing her arms around Andy. "We saved the Chronosphere!"

Andy let out a breath he didn't realize he was holding. "Phew! That was some wild ride through time, wasn't it?"

As they returned to the central chamber, the Lumina Bird greeted them with a nod of approval. "You have shown great wisdom and foresight," it said. "But the final trial awaits you now—the Trial of Compassion."

Tara squared her shoulders, her face set with determination. Just as she and the Lumina Bird approached The Bronze Passage of Trials, a cold, mocking laugh filled the air. From the shadows stepped Lord Nightweaver, his dark form towering, eyes glowing with a cruel light.

"Enough of these silly games!" Nightweaver snarled, his voice dripping with menace. "Taranterra will belong to the darkness, and no trials can save it from its fate!"

With a flick of his shadowy legs, Nightweaver summoned a swarm of shadow creatures. They poured from the darkness like a flood, their inky bodies stretching and twisting, blocking out the light.

"Quick! Through the door!" the Lumina Bird urged, its voice tense.

Tara hesitated, looking back at her friends. Toby and Andy stood firm, even though the shadow creatures were closing in fast. "Go on, Tara!" Toby called out, a fierce grin on his face. "We'll hold these creeps off. Finish the job!"

Andy gave her a thumbs-up, his wings buzzing with energy. "Give it everything you've got, Princess! We've got your back!"

Tara's heart ached to leave them, but she knew what she had to do. With a nod to her friends, she dashed through The Bronze Passage of Trials, the Lumina Bird flying close beside her. The sounds of the battle behind them faded away, leaving them in a place of quiet beauty.

They found themselves in a serene grove, bathed in soft twilight. At the center of the grove was a still, crystal-clear pool, its surface like a perfect mirror. Tara knew, deep down, that this trial would be different—it was not about strength or cleverness, but something deeper.

This was the Trial of Compassion, and it was the key to Taranterra's true destiny. The grove was quiet, the air filled with a soft glow from the Lumina Bird, who hovered beside her. "This is the Pool of Reflection," the Lumina Bird said in a calm, steady voice. "It shows the truth in the hearts of others—even your enemies. But be careful, Princess. The truth isn't always easy to accept."

Tara felt a shiver run down her spine as she stepped closer to the pool, her eyes fixed on its mirror-like surface. She took a deep breath and looked into the water. At first, there was nothing. But then, shapes started to form, slowly turning into images that sent a chill straight to her bones.

She saw Lord Nightweaver, but not as the dark villain she had come to fear. Instead, he appeared as a young spider, eyes filled with hope and determination. She watched him dream of protecting Taranterra, of creating a place where he and others like him could belong. But then, she saw the dreams turn dark, twisted by fear and loneliness. Nightweaver and the Shadow Weavers had once tried to do good, but they were afraid of being forgotten, lost in a world that was growing brighter without them.

Tara's throat tightened, her eyes welling with tears. "They're not evil," she whispered, her voice cracking. "They're lost."

The Lumina Bird nodded slowly, its eyes filled with sorrow. "Now you understand, Princess Tara," it said gently. "Your true task is not to defeat the Shadow Weavers. It is to heal them, to guide them back into the light."

Tara took a deep breath, the weight of what she had seen settling into her heart. She knew what she had to do. Turning away from the pool, she hurried back toward the bronze door, the Lumina Bird flying at her side.

When they stepped back into the central chamber, chaos awaited them. Shadow creatures filled the air like a storm of darkness, their inky forms twisting and thrashing. Toby and Andy were in the thick of it, fighting with everything they had, but the shadows seemed endless.

And there, towering above it all, was Lord Nightweaver, his power swelling with every passing second, feeding off the fear in the room.

Tara's heart pounded in her chest, but this time, it wasn't with fear—it was with determination. She stepped forward, the Cloak of Shadows wrapped around her shoulders. But something had changed; the cloak now glowed with a soft, golden light, like the first rays of dawn.

"Lord Nightweaver!" Tara called out, her voice strong and clear. "This battle isn't the answer. I've seen the truth in your heart, in all the hearts of the Shadow Weavers. You weren't meant to bring only darkness. You are the guardians of twilight, the keepers of dreams, the protectors of the shadows that make the light shine brighter."

Nightweaver's eyes flickered, confusion rippling across his face. "What trick is this?" he spat, but there was doubt in his voice now, a crack in his anger.

"It's no trick," Tara said, her voice softer now, filled with understanding. "You were afraid of being forgotten, of losing your place in a world that kept growing brighter. But don't you see? Taranterra needs the night as much as it needs the day. We need you—not as conquerors, but as protectors of the balance."

As Tara spoke, the glow from the Cloak of Shadows grew even brighter, turning into the Cloak of Twilight, its light spreading out like a warm embrace. It surrounded Tara and her friends, pushing back the darkness, creating a space where light and shadow stood side by side.

Nightweaver staggered, his shadowy form shaking. "No!" he shouted, his voice breaking. "The Cloak of Shadows cannot be used against us!"

Tara took a step closer, her eyes locked on his. "It's not against you," she said gently. "It's here to remind you of who you really are."

Then, with a deep breath, Tara began to weave. She didn't spin a web this time but something far more powerful—a tapestry of light and shadow, each thread telling a story. The scenes in the tapestry showed Taranterra's history, moments of joy and sorrow, of darkness and light intertwined. And in each scene, the Shadow Weavers appeared—not as villains, but as guardians, protectors of the balance between night and day.

"Look, Nightweaver," Tara said, her voice trembling with emotion. "You were never meant to live in darkness alone. Taranterra needs both light and shadow to thrive. An eternal night would destroy everything—even you."

For the first time, real uncertainty filled Nightweaver's eyes. His hands trembled, the darkness around him flickering like a dying flame. Some of the shadow creatures paused in their attack, drawn to the beauty of Tara's tapestry, their forms wavering as if remembering something they had long forgotten.

Seizing the moment, Tara raised the Whisperwind Flute to her lips. She played a melody that filled the air, a song of hope, of healing, of new beginnings. It was the kind of song that spoke of dawn after the darkest night, of forgiveness, of finding your way back home.

The light from the Cloak of Twilight grew even brighter, spreading across the chamber, touching every shadow creature. One by one, they began to change, their forms softening, their eyes filling with light. They weren't just creatures of darkness anymore—they were part of Taranterra's heart, guardians of dreams and twilight.

Nightweaver fell to his knees, his face a mix of sorrow and relief. "How?" he whispered, looking up at Tara with eyes that no longer glowed with anger but with something closer to understanding. "How did you do this?"

Tara knelt beside him, placing a hand gently on his arm. "You were never truly lost," she said softly. "You were just waiting for someone to remind you that even the darkest night can lead to the most beautiful dawn."

As the last note of the Whisperwind Flute faded into the air, the chamber glowed with a light that was both soft and strong—a light that embraced the shadows, not to banish them, but to live beside them. For in Taranterra, there would always be a place where light and shadow danced together, where day and night met as friends.

Nightweaver looked up at her, a flicker of hope crossing his face. "I remember now," he whispered, almost to himself. "We were supposed to protect the twilight, the moment where day and night meet. But we got lost, afraid we'd be forgotten in a world that kept getting brighter."

Tara reached out and gently placed her hand on Nightweaver's arm. "It's not too late," she said, her voice filled with warmth. "Taranterra needs both light and dark to thrive. Will you help us restore the balance?"

Nightweaver's eyes glistened, and with a humble bow of his head, he said, "Princess Tara, your compassion has shown me the truth. The Twilight Weavers are at your service."

Just then, the massive portal at the center of the chamber began to shimmer, its purple glow fading to a soft, silvery light that seemed to welcome them. It was no longer the gateway to a realm of shadows but something entirely different.

"Look!" Toby shouted, his face lighting up with excitement. "The portal's changing!"

Andy adjusted his goggles, leaning forward in awe. "This isn't a doorway to darkness anymore," he said, almost breathless. "It's a passage to... to..."

The portal shimmered and twisted, its glowing edges dissolving into a soft, golden light that spilled across the cave floor like the first rays of morning. Tara stepped closer, her heart thudding in her chest, as two familiar figures began to take shape within the glowing mist.

They weren't solid, not entirely. Their forms flickered like the glow of moonlight reflected on water—more memory than reality. A soft hum filled the air, like a lullaby sung by the wind.

Before Tara could speak, the two figures—the king and queen of Taranterra—stepped forward, their bodies glowing gently with threads of gold woven through their silky forms. Their eyes sparkled with warmth, carrying the weight of love and pride, and something deeper—an unspoken sorrow that made Tara's breath catch in her throat.

The queen was the first to speak, her voice soft but filled with strength. "Tara, our brave one. You may not know us yet, but we have always known you."

The king smiled gently, his many eyes twinkling with kindness. "We are your parents, Tara—your true parents. And we've waited for this moment since the day we had to let you go."

Tara's legs trembled beneath her as a wave of emotions crashed over her—confusion, disbelief, hope. "Mom? Dad?" she whispered, her voice fragile and cracked. She reached toward them instinctively, but her legs passed through their glowing forms like mist.

The queen's smile softened, and there was a glimmer of sadness in her eyes. "We are only a memory, my love. A piece of us stored here, waiting for the moment you would come home."

Tara's breath hitched. "You mean… you're not really here?"

The king's expression was gentle but steady. "No, my little one. We've been gone for a long time. But our love for you—our hope for you—has always remained."

Tara blinked, tears gathering at the edges of her eyes. "I never even got to meet you... I—" She choked on her words, unable to finish the thought.

The queen's gaze was full of understanding. "We may not have been there to watch you grow, but you were never alone, Tara. Mr. and Mrs. Webber—your foster parents—loved you as their own. They gave you a home, a place to belong, when we no longer could. And we are so grateful for that."

The king nodded, his voice steady and kind. "They didn't just raise you—they helped shape you into the leader you are now. Their love gave you roots, Tara. And it's those roots that have carried you through this journey."

Tara let out a shaky breath, her mind spinning with the enormity of their words. She had spent so much of her life feeling out of place, different—like she didn't belong anywhere. And now, here were her parents, telling her that she had always been right where she was meant to be.

The queen's voice was soft but filled with quiet strength. "Being a leader isn't about power or perfection, Tara. It's about knowing when to be strong and when to be gentle. It's about listening when others are silent and lifting them when they fall. It's about being brave enough to embrace the parts of yourself that are still growing."

The king leaned closer, his gaze warm. "And it's about knowing that you don't have to do it alone. Real strength lies in the bonds you make with others. The Webbers, your friends—they've walked beside you because they believe in you, just as we do."

Tara's heart swelled, the weight of their words settling over her like a warm blanket. For so long, she had been trying to prove herself, to live up to expectations she hadn't even fully understood. But now, standing here with the memory of her parents, she realized she didn't need to prove anything. She just needed to be herself.

A soft silence fell between them, heavy with meaning. Tara looked at them, her voice thick with emotion. "I never said thank you," she whispered, tears streaming down her face.

The queen smiled, her form beginning to flicker as the magic that held them here started to fade. "You'll never have to, my love. Our hearts have always known."

The king gave her a final, gentle look. "We are so proud of you, Tara. Keep going. The light inside you will guide Taranterra to a brighter future."

Their glowing forms shimmered, becoming thinner, like threads of silk unraveling in the wind.

"No—please don't go," Tara whispered, her voice cracking. She reached out again, even though she knew she couldn't hold onto them.

The queen's smile remained, soft and full of love. "We are always with you, Tara. In every step you take, in every choice you make—we will be there."

And then, with one last flicker of golden light, they were gone, leaving only the faint hum of magic in the air and the warmth of their words in Tara's heart.

Tara stood in silence for a moment, her tears falling freely. She didn't try to stop them—she let them fall, not from sadness, but from a bittersweet joy. Her parents might be gone, but she carried their love with her. She always had.

Taking a deep breath, Tara straightened her legs, a quiet resolve blooming inside her. She wasn't just a lost princess anymore. She was a leader—one who understood the power of love, of friendship, of roots that ran deep.

Tara stood still, the weight of her parents' words settling into her heart like the roots of a tree, deep and steady. She wiped her face with one leg, her breath uneven but lighter somehow, as if the burden she'd carried for so long had shifted into something she could finally hold without it breaking her.

Then she heard a soft cough behind her.

"So… you okay there, Princess?" Toby asked gently, stepping closer. His usual playful grin was gone, replaced by something quieter—softer. "You've been through a lot. I mean, I've seen webs with fewer knots than you've had to untangle tonight."

Tara gave a shaky laugh, still catching her breath. "Yeah. I think I am, Toby. For the first time in a long time… I think I am."

Toby's expression softened even further, and he tilted his head just slightly. "You know," he began, his voice low and teasing, "if you weren't so busy saving the world, I might've kissed you right about now."

Tara blinked at him, taken aback for a second before bursting into laughter, the sound bubbling up from somewhere deep inside her. She swatted his shoulder with one leg. "Toby, you're impossible."

"Yeah, but you like me anyway." Toby winked, his grin slipping back into place, the familiar spark returning to his eyes. Then, more quietly, he added, "And I like you too, Tara. You've been carrying so much all this time, and somehow you kept walking through it, like the badass I always knew you were."

Tara gave him a fond look, her heart lighter than it had been in days. "I couldn't have done any of it without you, Toby. Thank you."

Toby gave a playful bow, one leg sweeping dramatically. "Of course, Your Majesty. Anytime you need someone to make terrible jokes or flirt inappropriately in the middle of life-threatening situations, I'll be there."

Then Andy shuffled closer, his usual quirky grin a little hesitant, as if unsure of where he fit into this moment. "So, uh… I'm guessing this is the part where you two do some emotional soul-bonding thing, and I quietly sneak away before it gets too sappy?"

Tara turned toward him, her gaze soft but steady. "You're not sneaking away, Andy."

Andy blinked, his grin faltering for a second. "Oh. I mean, I'm more of the new guy... wasn't sure if I'm, you know, officially part of the team yet."

Tara stepped closer, giving him a reassuring look. "You saved my life, Andy. You're stuck with us now."

Andy's smile returned, though it was smaller, almost shy. "Well, I've gotta say, I don't mind being stuck. You two are... not the worst company."

"Not the worst?" Toby gasped, clutching his chest in mock offense. "We're legendary company."

"Fine," Andy relented, adjusting his goggles with an exaggerated flourish. "You're slightly above average. Happy?"

"Ecstatic," Toby replied with a wink. "And just so you know, Andy, I expect you to invent some mind-blowing gadgets the next time we run into trouble."

"Oh, no pressure," Andy shot back, smirking. "Just save the world, crack jokes, and blow stuff up in style. Easy."

Tara watched the two of them banter, a smile playing on her lips. The sadness of her parents' memory lingered, but it wasn't heavy anymore—it was something precious, something she carried alongside the friendship she had built with these two ridiculous spiders.

"You know," Tara said, her voice warm, "I think we're going to be okay."

Toby shot her a cheeky grin. "Yeah? Well, I knew that the moment you didn't punch me for flirting with you."

"Don't test me, Toby," Tara warned playfully, though her smile never faded.

Andy laughed, the kind of laugh that only comes when you know you've found something real. "Well, this might not have been the adventure I signed up for, but... I think it's the one I needed."

Tara gave both of them a grateful look. "Me too. I couldn't have done this alone. Thank you, both of you."

Toby threw one of his front legs around Andy's shoulders. "Get used to it, Andy. Emotional speeches and heroic nonsense are part of the package."

Andy huffed, pretending to be annoyed, though his grin said otherwise. "Fine, but I'm still calling dibs on blowing something up next time."

Tara rolled her eyes, but the warmth in her heart stayed with her, steady and true. With these two by her side—Toby's relentless humor and Andy's chaotic brilliance—she knew she wasn't just facing the future as a princess. She was facing it with friends who would walk with her, no matter what came next.

And that, she realized, was more than enough.

With a deep breath and a new sense of purpose, Tara turned toward the path ahead. "Let's go," she said. "Taranterra's waiting."

Toby gave a little salute. "Lead the way, Princess. We've got your back."

Andy adjusted his goggles with a grin. "And I've got the explosions. Just in case."

Suddenly, everything around her began to blur, the scene fading into a soft, swirling mist. She heard a voice calling her name, but it seemed distant, far away.

"Miss Tara," the voice repeated, clearer now. "We're late. You need to go on stage."

Tara's eyes blinked open, the world of Taranterra dissolving into the bright lights of a small, modern room. She was sitting on a chair, her reflection staring back at her from a large mirror. Standing in front of her was a young man with a concerned look on his face. It was Toby—no longer a bouncing spider but her human assistant, holding a clipboard.

"Is everything okay?" Toby asked, his brow creased with worry. "You seemed far away."

Tara shook her head, still trying to shake the feeling of the dream. "I'm fine, Toby," she said with a small smile. "Just... had a pretty intense dream, that's all. Don't worry, I'm ready now."

She stood up, straightened her coat, and walked out of the green room. The world of Taranterra still lingered in her mind, but now she was back in the present, in the world she knew. As she stepped onto the stage, the sound of applause filled the room—a sea of 1,330 people clapping, their faces turned toward her.

The bright lights of the TED Talk stage illuminated her, and she heard the emcee's voice echo through the hall. "Welcome to TED Talk, Miss Tara, the youngest successful entrepreneur."

Tara took the microphone, her eyes sweeping over the audience. For a moment, the faces seemed to blend into the glowing eyes of the Twilight Weavers, the warmth of her parents' embrace still fresh in her heart. Then, with a confident smile, she looked up and spoke.

"Thank you all for being here," she began, her voice steady, filled with the kind of warmth that comes from hard-earned lessons. "I have a story to share. Not just about building a business, but about what it really means to lead. And spoiler alert—it's not about having all the answers."

The crowd chuckled softly, leaning in, caught by the sincerity in her tone. Tara took a deep breath, letting the rhythm of the moment guide her.

"You see," she continued, "for a long time, I thought leadership was about perfection—about never making mistakes, always knowing the way forward. But it turns out, real leadership is something else entirely. It's about learning to trust the people around you. It's about finding light, even when everything feels dark. And, most importantly, it's about realizing that no one gets through it alone."

Her mind drifted briefly to Andy, with his chaotic brilliance and endless optimism, and Toby, who had always known exactly when to joke and when to show up with quiet support. They had been with her every step of the way, just like her foster parents—the Webbers—had been, too.

Tara paused for a second, scanning the room, feeling the energy of the audience. "I wasn't always ready for what life threw at me," she admitted, a small smile tugging at her lips. "But I learned something important: You don't have to be perfect to start. You just have to begin."

The applause swelled, soft and encouraging, like a gentle wave, but Tara wasn't finished.

"My journey was never about being a lone hero. It was about the connections I made—the people who believed in me when I couldn't believe in myself. And that's what makes any adventure worth taking." She glanced toward the side of the stage, catching Toby's gaze. His smile was small but knowing, as if saying, You've got this.

"To everyone out there," Tara continued, "whether you're starting a new journey, running a business, or simply trying to find your way—know this: the light you carry inside is enough. And the people who walk beside you? They're your real strength."

For a moment, she swore she felt the warmth of her parents' presence, the memory of their final words settling over her like a quiet promise. "You'll never have to say thank you."

Tara blinked, holding back the tears that threatened to rise. Instead, she smiled—wide, genuine, and filled with the kind of hope that can only come from knowing you're exactly where you need to be.

"And before I go," she said, her voice light but deliberate, "there's one more thing I've learned on this journey: Life's too short not to have a little fun along the way."

The crowd chuckled again, some leaning in closer, waiting for what was next.

"So," she added with a playful grin, "let me leave you with this: If you ever find yourself bouncing from mushroom to mushroom in a glowing forest, trust the mushrooms. And more importantly, trust yourself."

The room erupted into laughter, applause bursting like fireworks around her. Tara felt the weight of the moment lift, replaced with something lighter—something right.

She gave one last glance toward Toby, who gave her a thumbs-up, the same old glint of mischief in his eyes.

We've got this, she thought, feeling the threads of her life—both real and imagined—woven tightly together.

As the applause washed over her, Tara knew with absolute certainty that her adventure wasn't over. It was only just beginning.

www.ingramcontent.com/pod-product-compliance
Lightning Source LLC
LaVergne TN
LVHW041105150826
845673LV00007B/1939

* 9 7 9 8 8 9 6 3 2 7 1 4 1 *